PROMISED VIRGINS

PROMISED VIRGINS

A NOVEL OF JIHAD

JEFFREY FLEISHMAN

ARCADE PUBLISHING • NEW YORK

FIRST EDITION

This is a work of fiction. Names, characters, places, and incidents are
either the work of the author's imagination or are used fictitiously.

Library of Congress Cataloging-in-Publication Data

Fleishman, Jeffrey.
  Promised virgins : a novel of Jihad / Jeffrey Fleishman. —1st ed.
    p. cm.
  ISBN 978-1-55970-897-5 (alk. paper)
  1. Journalists—United States—Fiction. 2. Americans—Balkan Penin-
sula—Fiction. 3. Kosovo War, 1998–1999—Fiction. 4. Kosovo (Repub-
lic)—Ethnic relations—Fiction. 5. Terrorists—Fiction. 6. Jihad—Fiction.
I. Title.

  PS3606.L457P76 2009
  813'.6—dc22   2008031205

Published in the United States by Arcade Publishing, Inc., New York
Distributed by Hachette Book Group USA

Visit our Web site at www.arcadepub.com

10 9 8 7 6 5 4 3 2 1

Designed by API

EB

PRINTED IN THE UNITED STATES OF AMERICA

For Clare

PROMISED VIRGINS

Chapter 1

She climbs into bed with death in her hair. She tried to scrub it out, but we had only bottled water and little shampoo. She washed and washed, and cried and cursed in that strange and staccato language of hers, but still it lingers, acid beneath apricots. There is no electricity and no moon. She slips beside me. Her damp, haunted hair — she calls it possessed, says it whispers with ghosts — brushes me like a cool sheet.

Helicopters skitter against the night sky. Rain blows hard and sideways, drumming our windows and softening the rattle of firefights across the city; they burst like match strikes, quick flames of bullets, then diminishment. Then another. And another. Years ago I rushed toward them, a wild scribe with a pencil and notebook, trailing the phosphorous glow and crackle of street battles until dawn. A sweet addiction it was to inhale the tang of gunpowder, to hear the scrape of boots in glinted alleys. But I am older. More discriminating, I suppose, in what qualifies as news. My ears are attuned to atrocity. I can tell by the hum of a Kalashnikov and the murmur of graveside prayers what will land on the front page and what will fall deep inside the newspaper. I have learned things. A baby in a snowsuit with a slit throat scattered amid bodies in a burning village: that's page one. A girl gang-raped before her first period: page one, below the fold. A few dead guerrillas splayed in a roadside gully are at best A-9 or mental notes to be stored and recalled for color in one of those grand wartime Sunday stories editors like so much. The Sunday piece is the flaunt of my trade: big and windy, it takes faithful subscribers to the madness beyond their cul-de-sacs. There is a twitch of irony in that thought, but I am not bitter. I am here to write for the American reader whose attention span for strange-sounding surnames and distant lands is enchantingly short. I will not judge. I will tell only what I see. The righteousness and indignation, the moral values, as it were, I leave to others.

My story, the one I led with, the one involving the girl with the tormented hair, is set a few years before those planes sliced into the silver towers and spoiled the skyline of New York. Remember all those silly, whining headlines: WHY DO THEY HATE US? A ridiculous, rhetorical question, ripe with the victim's denial of his own sin. But who knew there could be so much tattered paper? Shreds floating, flickering, and gliding, as if ripped from a paper sky and blown from the palms of God. The girder-groan and the crumple and the storm of glass and all those bits of data, the insurance annuities and the stock analyses, the actuaries and the portfolios, the arcane keystrokes of a people obliterated in billows of blood-speckled confetti. And the smoke. Hanging for days and seeping like strange, gray paint across the horizon, so many shades of gray you never knew existed, gray like metal, ash, mackerel, nickels, shale, gray like rain on power plants, gray subtle and narrow, blushed and smeared, gray like a footprint in a hallway or that hushed gasp when dusk succumbs to night. No matter. It's done; the names of the innocent scratched in stone and recited like poems along the river. I didn't anticipate it either, at least not such a simple plan for destruction, even though for a brief time I was among it in a war that jerked like a top spinning through a small country with a hard-to-pronounce name. There are so many tempests out there.

Alija sits up and ties back her hair.

"Did we decide how many there were?"

"Sixty-nine."

"The rows were uneven."

"I counted twice. Sixty-nine."

"I only saw a few shovels."

"They worked through the night."

"Did you see that TV guy doing his stand-up on the fresh dirt of the grave? The family was still crying over it. Bastard."

"Everything's a prop for TV."

"How will I get this out of my hair?"

"It's in our clothes too. I wrote naked."

"I hate this smell. We go out every day, and every day I come back with other people's death on me."

"The fighting's getting worse."

"It's late summer. Autumn will cover the scent."

"The snow will help."

"I don't want war in winter."

"Any word on your brother?"

"Nothing."

Alija sleeps. The dead are buried in uneven rows. Why should death be any more precise than life? Sixty-nine bodies untangled from a shallow mass grave discovered when a child ran across a field to pick what he thought was a silver-black flower rippling like a flame from the earth. It was a woman's scarf. The rest of her lay beneath, twisted together with the others. Alija studied their pallid faces, looking for her brother. Each body was taken and washed, water and wounds and half-rotted flesh. There was not much time for religion or calling Allah. The mortars came quickly, as they often did, exploding in thistle, kneading and softening the land, leaving rips across the fields. Blackbirds swirled like cinders in the sky, and, when the afternoon was streaked with enough metal, the guerrillas and the army paused for beer and tea and a little porn, and the villagers hustled their dead up the hillside, hammered wooden markers into the earth, and disappeared as dusk played tricks in the mountains. The gravediggers stayed. Page one.

I hear Brian Conrad before he knocks. A jangle of journalistic ingenuity, he despises war yet appears time and again, traipsing in big boots and carrying a fountain pen to the edge of battle. He is my shadow, my bookmark: a man whose presence tells me that I am in the right place. I hadn't seen him for months. Alija and I glimpsed him from a distance earlier at the graveyard, but he was gone before we reached him, racing no doubt toward some shred of half-heard possibility that may find its way into a story or just as likely be discarded. Brian draws energy from chaos and is seldom tired

4

at the end of a long day. He writes with abandon, fearful that if he contemplated too much the words would run away; his fingers, bitten at the nails, move over the keys like a dance troupe on speed. His notebooks — dirty and fat and brittle from rain — are full of interviews, conspiracies, and ramblings. He'll never use most of it. For Brian, the joy is collecting. Information is ephemeral. A screed written in a cloud, a love letter scrawled in sand. Brian says humans want accuracy but, like a Jew with a rosary in his hands, don't know what to make of it. Accuracy brings no end to suffering; it bewilders more than it comforts. I've often wondered, though, what treasures are scribbled on those notebook pages, what stories and secrets his editors will never know.

"Jay, you awake?"

"What do you think? Shhhh. Alija's sleeping."

"Can I use your sat phone? Mine just died."

"I only have a little battery left."

"Just gotta send."

I light a candle. He unfolds his computer.

"Some scene today, huh? Hey, you got any whiskey?"

"A little raki, but it's rotgut."

"I'll just have a swallow then. How many graves did you count?"

"Sixty-nine."

"Shit. I wrote seventy."

"I counted sixty-nine."

"Jesus, it never fails."

"I'm staying with sixty-nine."

"How long you in this time?"

"A few months, maybe. You?"

"I don't know. I almost got shot two days ago out near Djakovica. Drove right into a firefight. My translator froze. I gotta get a new translator. My guy's too nervous, crazy darting eyes. Does Alija know anybody?"

"I'll ask."

"Pour me a little more raki."

The satellite phone finds its bead. Brian's story flashes across his computer screen and careens into space to be collected thousands of miles away in a peaceful city where electricity hums all night and women's hair smells of lilac or some synthesized mix of herbs, musk, and bottled flowers. It is an amazing world that can devise something as fine as the satellite phone. All the restless blips on wars, stock markets, crime, melting polar ice caps, starving children, trapped coal miners, lost fishermen, nuclear warheads, infidelities, football scores, potato-chip sales, medical breakthroughs, and the mea culpas of preachers and politicians — all that stuff running in invisible electric rivers across the universe. Millions of genies escaped from bottles shimmering beyond us, circumnavigating our perceptions and then returning to us, grits of knowledge collected and stored in Pentium configurations. I mention this to Brian. He looks at his raki.

"I'd trade my left nut for a good sat phone. What's the first thing we do when we get to a shit hole like this? Hook up the computer to the sat phone to make sure we're connected. Every night wondering if that magic is gonna work again. What if some cosmic storm blows away my satellite? My story lost in static, going nowhere."

"You're only as good as your Thrane and Thrane."

"They have these smaller ones now. Thurayas. They look like cell phones on steroids. So what's up with you and Alija?"

"Not much."

"C'mon, Jay, cardinal rule. Never sleep with your translator. Rarely ends pretty."

"No comment."

"All right, I used your sat phone and emptied your raki. My work here is done. I'm going to bed."

"Your editors going to like your story?"

"Don't mention editors. I've got enough problems."

He leaves, down the stairs and scuffing the street, his laptop under his arm in the hour before dawn.

I do sleep with Alija. I feel her skin on mine; I smell the sweet acridity of her hair. But I have never been inside her. I have never felt her close around me, even on those nights when weariness and liquor nudge the restless together. Why? Such revelations are best left till later. If I divulge now, it will color what's to come. This is an adventure story. I am searching for a man in the mountains. He has a beard and bandoliers crisscrossing his chest. He has cracked hands and muddy boots. I have never seen him. This is what I hear: he is new to the war. He slipped into the mountains, changed the dynamics of things. Villagers whisper about his eyes; they say they are hard and black and luminous. Boys want to be him, and already there is myth in the mountains. I am not fond of that word. It is overused bullshit for lazy journalists. *Myth* is for starlight and gods playing games in the clouds; it is the intangible mystery of spirit and imagination that should not be confused with the world's coarser designs. But I will say this, myth in war is as lethal as artillery. Dangerous to all sides.

They say this man brought with him five donkeys loaded with bullets, guns, plastic explosives, bricks of money, a few computers, and hundreds of pounds of dates. The Prophet Mohammed ate dates to strengthen himself before battle, and if this is a symbol, then this is a man I need to find. It's strange. Most guerrillas here are not religious. Mohammed to them is an outline, not a purpose. Their zeal is for land and crops and business. A few leaders among them peddle crudely embroidered manifestos of socialism and democracy. They yammer on until you go numb. I have little patience for guerrilla intellectuals quoting — and, I must note, badly quoting — a universe of gurus and thinkers from Marx to Mao to Jefferson to Nietzsche in convolutions that will only screw their country up more than it's screwed up now. The masses don't want eloquence; they want the plumbing to work and the lights to come on at night. Give me a rebel who just wants to kill his enemy and return to his family, and I'll show you a man or, these days, a woman whose vision is pure.

Alija sleeps. I am tired. My eyes closed, I cannot dream. Let us go to the time before the millennium when a White House intern saved the smudge on her dress and a bearded man with a different God led a ragged legion across the thrum of Europe. Listen.

Chapter 2

I know a secret. Language is a weapon in war. Concealing and unmasking, it targets identity. Faces, hands, a smile, the cut of an eye, these tell you little. The enemy hides in vowels and syllables, the hardness of a consonant, the tender inflection, the spin and whirl of nuance. My language tells you how I hate and how I love, how far I would go to slit your throat and burn your body. Words are invisible armies, playing and dancing, moving like lethal ripples through fields of winter grass. I have learned this.

The language game unfolds at the military checkpoint. Razor wire and raki and pissed-off Serb interior police. They are called the MUP, big bastards in blue-and-gray jumpsuits with black-barreled Kalashnikovs, knives, and high-caliber machine guns. They own the roads. They are the gatekeepers — the ferrymen of Hades, if you will — to battles and rumored atrocities. They can shoot you. They can wave you away, or they can let you pass across the flatlands and into the mountains. Sometimes they give you a speeding ticket just for the surreal hell of it. I need to get beyond them to find the bearded man with the dates.

Alija closes her eyes as we approach the checkpoint. It is ritual. The barrel of a 9mm clicks on the window. We are here. Alija opens her eyes and she is someone else. She speaks to the MUP, her words slow and throaty. She mimics the sounds of his tongue. She tosses them like stone. Thick-faced and newly shaven, the MUP listens, waiting for that crack, that tear in the verbal tissue that will reveal that Alija, despite her black hair and fair skin and perfect accent, is not a Serb, that she is Albanian, the enemy. Trash. He takes my passport.

"Where you from?" he says to Alija.

"Pristina."

"Pristina. What neighborhood?"

She doesn't answer.

"How do you live with those Albanian cocksuckers?"

"It's no problem."

"We'll kill them all, you know?"

She doesn't answer.

"What's wrong? You like Albanians? You fucking Albanians?"

She doesn't answer. He leans into the car, brushing the gun barrel through her hair.

"You're beautiful," he says. "A nice mouth. Why are you working with this American propagandist?"

Propagandist. Jesus, this dumb ass thinks we're still in the Cold War. Someone wake him up and boot him into the new world order, which decidedly is breaking down. But it's guys like him who throw the gearbox into neutral, diverting chaos to places where it shouldn't be, taking energy away from places that need it and gumming us all into a mess because he won't buy a map and run his fingers over new geographies. I decide to keep my rumination to myself. He waves his gun toward me, then back to Alija. Two other MUP raise Kalashnikovs. A fourth approaches the Jeep and snarls into a walkie-talkie. The armored personnel carrier near the ditch swings its turret toward us. Farmers hauling vegetable sacks shuffle for cover, and the blackbirds in the trees follow rifle glints and wait for a crack to startle them into flight. It is loud but quiet, like the space between crescendo and solo clarinet, one mood slipping into another and another in a chain reaction of unpredictable composition. These are the times you wish you were a loan officer or a claims adjuster, squirting mustard on a hot dog and pondering Wal-Mart vastness at a backyard cookout in a suburb in one of those fine American towns.

"You know," says the MUP at Alija's window, "you might be Albanian. You trying to fool me? One way to tell."

He laughs and whispers to her. He stands back from the jeep, grabs his crotch, and waves us on. I accelerate, waiting for the bullet through the back window. I check the rearview. Rifles are lowered, cigarettes are passed, someone spits. The crazy MUP storm is over. We head toward the fighting in the distance.

"That was as nasty as rush hour on the Brooklyn Bridge." Alija doesn't smile. She doesn't get it. Maybe the world is too big. Someone's icon is another's mystery; someone's folklore another's atrocity. Alija's tears don't drop. They are dried by wind rushing in from the fields, where boys with horse plows plant land mines and wheat in crooked rows beneath the sun.

"We may not find him today."

"I know."

"You always want it now. The first one there. Don't get pissed if someone finds him before we do. It's hard. Look at those mountains. Where is he?"

"It may take a while," I say.

"I wonder who he is."

"I don't know his name."

"I heard it's Suli. But that's not certain. Some say he came from Chechnya. Others claim he's from the Sudan. They say he speaks of infidels and fire."

"An Allah's boy. You think that will sell here?"

"I don't know. You Americans haven't helped. We've listened to your promises of human rights and, what's that famous phrase, oh yeah, *self-determination* for a decade. Americans sound pretty on paper."

"Sound bites. Americans give good sound bite."

"Good talkers."

"Your English is softer these days, more delicate."

"Haven't you noticed I've been watching CDs of British movies on your laptop? You can get anything on the black market now. I like the American accent, but the Brits know how to pronounce. They hold on to the word."

"You weren't so uppity when we met."

"I was watching Hollywood back then. Scorsese. You know, 'Where's my money, you fucking low-rent piece of shit?'"

"That's it. Poetry!"

"I'm more . . . Oh, what's that word?"

"Cultured?"

"No. *Refined.* That's it. I'm more refined these days."

In a mock British accent, Alija says, "Would you be so kind as to pass the bullets? And please, do tell John to stop by for a spot of brandy after the massacre."

She laughs.

We stop at a house. Alija knocks. A boy peers through a crack in the door and lets us in. He hugs Alija and asks for candy. He whirls around her like a breeze around a pole. She hands him a gumdrop and kisses him on the forehead. The place smells of onions and kerosene, and the kid vanishes and a slender man with deep-set eyes and badly cut hair appears. He wears an old cardigan and baggy pants and sits beneath a window in a slant of sunlight. He is a teacher in the school in the next village, and Alija tells me two of his brothers are guerrillas. They left home months ago, and they send news down from the mountains. The boy brings tea and sugar cubes. He throws wood into the stove and vanishes again. Children here do that. In an instant they can shift from omnipresence to ether. The man must be reading my mind.

"It's the war," he says. "Children must know when to become invisible."

He offers a cigarette. I decline.

"American?"

"Yes."

"Americans are funny. They grow the best tobacco, but they've stopped smoking."

"We are full of contradictions."

"The world has suffered because of them."

13

He looks at me, flicking ash off his sweater. "Alija says you want to know about the resistance."

"Yes."

"I don't know much. But it will last. It's the way now."

"Have you heard about this new man in the mountains? The one with the beard and dates?"

Alija stops the translation and glares at me. I am pushing too quickly. The man sits back in the sunlight. Interviews are tiny plays. They have pleasantries and climaxes, subplots and asides. To neglect one is to spoil the other. The man enjoys tea and conversation. I am pulling him faster than he wants to go. He needs intimacy. He needs to reveal what he knows layer by layer. Information here is cherished, hardwon, not easily surrendered to some nonsmoking American with a notebook. I know this. I pride myself on listening. Why, then, am I breaking cadence? Maybe I'm tired of this dance, tired of unraveling all the barbed secrets of dirt-house schoolteachers in war zones, tired of chasing information as if it's a lantern moving ahead of me from village to village. I wonder if the man knows I'm thinking this. I'm sitting across his table, stirring my tea and wondering what worth this man has for me. I don't want to be this way. I want to be enchanted; I want this man to unfold the story of his family, how he survives on this land, why he became a teacher, why his brothers picked up Kalashnikovs, and I want to know what will happen to the boy who opened the door and let us in.

I saw a man once in Africa. Rebels had just left his village. He stood in blood and dirt near the piled bodies of his family. He looked at me. He spoke no English. He pointed to his family and then he pointed to my notebook. His fingers were crooked as kindling. He moved his hand as if he were writing against the sky. He wanted it recorded. Somewhere, on some scrap of paper, he wanted words for all that had been taken. But there were a lot of villages just like his, a lot of stacked bodies, and when I sat down to write the story that night on the banks of a tributary feeding the Congo River, the man who scrawled his hand across the horizon never made it into my copy, his family's fate chronicled by obscurity.

Alija says good-bye to the teacher. She gets into the Jeep. Slams the door.

"You went too fast."

"I know."

"Don't do that again. If you do, you'll never find the man you're looking for."

"You've reverted to Scorsese."

"Screw that, Jay, you know what I mean."

It's nearing dusk and we need a place to sleep. We drive to another village, or rather a knot of houses near a stream. We stop at one with a small courtyard surrounded by a mud-brick wall. Another child, this time a girl, willows out of the gate, flickers around our Jeep, and vanishes. I park around back. Inside, the courtyard seems another world, a patch of green with gnarled grapevines and a long table beneath. An old man sits smoking a cigarette, and a woman, wearing a head scarf and moving with the ferocity of a bulldog, sweeps around the table. The man says, "Welcome." Cheese and bread and jam appear, delivered quietly by the girl. Alija winks and slips her a gumdrop. The woman brings tea, and we sit — the moon quarter-full in the sky — and talk among the candles. The man is not interested in war. He wants to know about Michael Jordan's jump shot and if I think it's possible for a Cadillac to navigate this land's winding dirt roads.

"I don't think a Cadillac would work here," says the man. "It rides too low and elegant."

"You always speak of Cadillacs," says the woman. "You have never touched one. You should worry more about your horse cart and tractor."

"I've seen plenty of Cadillacs on TV, in pictures." He bends toward me and whispers. "She doesn't like it when I explain about Cadillacs. She's jealous of the Cadillac."

He rolls another cigarette.

"It's cold," he says, gesturing toward Alija. "You two sleep in the kitchen near the stove."

The couple walks into the house, the woman first, and the man, with his stiff left leg, follows like an imperfect shadow. Alija and I stay at the table. The candles have nearly burned away; the moon has sharpened in the night.

"Do you think I'll find my brother?"

"Yes."

"It's been months."

"He may be hiding."

"All I know is that he left the house one morning. The MUP have been rounding up young men. Have you noticed there are fewer in the villages?"

"Many are in the mountains with the guerrillas. Would your brother fight?"

"I don't know. He's a university student. Students don't make good fighters."

"We'll keep looking."

"Maybe your man with the dates will know. This old man just told me he's heard the dateman has a camp two mountains from here. I know the place. There are caves high up."

"Tough for the MUP to attack."

"Nothing's too tough for the MUP."

"Maybe you should fight."

"I would be a good fighter." She laughs.

We go inside. Embers glow through cracks in the stove. I like what Alija said. "The dateman." I will call him the dateman. We throw blankets on the floor and sleep in our clothes.

Chapter 3

The morning's cool. We thank the old couple and leave, taking bread and fig jam the woman has tucked into our Jeep. Sheep scurry to grazing fields, and sunlight peels back fog. I love this twilight moment before life tramples clarity. I worked in a New Jersey factory years ago. Got up before dawn and drove through my patch of America in a time before I knew the intentions or even the existence of bearded men with dates and visions. How long had they been out there? Not known, T. S. Eliot once wrote, because not looked or listened for. But there were inklings, and every now and then there'd be a ripple of disturbance just violent and bloody enough to slip onto the news pages, create temporary concern, and then vanish as exotic anomaly; you registered it, pondered the brutality, counted the bodies, mouthed a few unpronounceable names, and turned the page. Imagine all the sounds and furious sermons running through those tiny anonymous desert and mountain wars that never reach the streets leading to my old factory. Alija points out the window. A small crowd of shepherds and farmers has gathered around a car stopped in front of us. A man and woman bicker in English across the hood, and the shepherds giggle, understanding the gist, if not the words.

"Let's go down this dirt road," says the woman.

"No way."

"C'mon. It'll save thirty minutes."

"Nope."

"C'mon."

"I'm not going. We don't know if it was mined last night."

"We'll go slow."

"No."

"Pussy. Ted, you're such a pussy."

Ted is agitated. But the woman is lovely. I might have followed her down a dirt road years ago. Faded jeans and a tight T-shirt, a bandana threading her hair, she is young and has that irritating Philadelphia Main Line patrician air of entitlement. Her lips are as slender as ribbons, her nose is like a razor. She is a daughter of money, seeking a break from the sanctuary she has lived in since birth. Her first or second war, I guess; she is still too naive to understand the things she should understand. This is my private conjecture game, sketching mental composites that, I must admit, mostly turn out to be true. Ted is a less complicated affair. A straightforward type, a guy whose smile doesn't always propel him as far as he'd like, which, whenever he is with the kind of woman he now faces across the hood, becomes sadly apparent. No matter. I know one thing for sure about both of them. They're freelancers, and they've spoiled my morning quiet and mussed up the clarity. Freelancers live on promises; they are journalism's bohemians and lost souls, hauling notebooks and beat-up computers across this battered planet. They wear their nerves outside their skin and appear wherever a story is hot, disappear before it cools. They are bees at a picnic. They dish news to papers in Cleveland and Pittsburgh — those places that want a foreign byline but wait months before paying the poor rent-a-hack in the war zone.

"Hi, guys," I say as Alija and I get out of the Jeep.

"Hey. I'm Ted. This is Ellen."

"I'm Jay, and this is my translator, Alija."

"You work for the *Herald*, right?" says Ellen.

"For the last fifteen years."

"I've read your stuff."

I love how Ellen ended that sentence. "Read your stuff." No assessment, just recognition. That's good.

"What are you doing up so early? Is there fighting somewhere?"

"I don't know. Alija and I just got an early start."

"Alija, is he telling the truth?"

"He mostly tells the truth."

"Do you think it's safe to go down the dirt road?" Ted says.

"If no one else has been down it this morning, you don't want to be the first."

"Mined, right?"

"Could be."

"I asked these shepherds," says Alija. "The MUP and the guerrillas were through here last night. Any one of them could have planted something."

"Let's buy a donkey off one of these guys," says Ellen. "We'll send it down the dirt road ahead of us."

"Blowing up a donkey's probably not a good idea around here."

"All right," Ellen says to Ted. "We'll go on the main road. It'll waste time and cut into our day. But let's just go."

Ellen slams the door, and she and Ted drive off.

"Weird chick," says Alija.

"I'd hate to be one of her pets."

"And you thought I was difficult."

"Who's that guy over there?"

"Where?"

"In the graveyard under the tree. See? Sitting with the Kalashnikov and shovel."

The man watches us walk across the road. He calls himself the Lion, but he lacks the majesty for such a title. A body rolled in linen lies in the shade next to him.

"My father," he says.

He rises and measures the ground with a willow branch. The shovel rips grass and breaks earth. The Lion had joined the guerrillas but was called home to bury his father, who died of pneumonia several days after the MUP set his village aflame and chased his family into the mountains. He points up the hill. I see the village and smell ash and charcoal. Overnight, hamlets turn to black smudges on this landscape, and amid the ruins bones as white as starlight poke through the blackened flesh of those not swift enough. Blood evaporates like water, but the bones of a half-burned body have a mesmerizing purity that glows against the dirt and the dust and the broken clay and fallen timber of a

21

house. The MUP torch what they cannot defeat, and with every fire more young men pour into the mountains with rifles and pitchforks. I have seen only two pitchforks, but pitchforks are like the dateman, images spun into myth. Maybe it's the sound. *Pitchfork.* Two harsh syllables that add a cadence to a sentence, not to mention the anachronistic conjuring. It's a good, strong word with a shade of ominous intent. *Pitchfork* works nicely in a lede. For some reason, journalists love this kind of stuff. The Lion digs. A thin line of muscles moves beneath his shirt. His sneakers are filled with soil and he works quickly, carving the walls of his father's grave, weeping sometimes and talking to himself. He looks at Alija.

"We have women fighters," he says.

"I think my brother may have joined, or he was taken by the MUP. I can't find him."

"We're scattered all over. What's his name?"

"Ardian. He just turned eighteen. He studies at university."

"Won't do him much good."

The Lion quiets, jumps out of the hole, and drags his father closer.

"Help me."

I grab the shoulders, and we lower the father into the ground. Through a rip I see the old man's face, a scrunched angry canvas of deep lines, gray stubble, and a protruding brow. I cannot see, but I'm sure he wears rubber galoshes and a tattered blazer, and somewhere in the death shroud there is a walking stick and at least one thing of value. A picture. A bank note. A letter mailed from a foreign land.

22

"My father created ten children, seven of them boys. He dug the deepest well in the village and kept the best sheep."

Dirt rattles the linen. The sound softens as the Lion fills the hole.

"Where's your marker?"

"I have none. I'll know where to find it. These are not days for grieving. We'll grieve when we have won."

These are the sentences you hear from a translator. Words distilled from one language and siphoned into another. Alija's good at it, but I'm sure some words and phrases never make the trip from one tongue to the next. Was the Lion really that poetic, or was there clutter amid the verse that fell into a limbo of syllables and clauses, spoken but lost forever? Alija's translation is direct, parsed of adjectives and flourish. She moves sentences like ships across the sea. "We'll grieve when we have won." As soon as it was uttered, I put a star next to it in my notebook and knew it would end up in a story.

"Who is your commander?" says Alija.

"Don't speak of such things. There are many commanders. We are strong."

"We heard about a new man."

The Lion smiles. "What have you heard?"

"That someone new has arrived. A foreigner who came on donkeys through the mountains."

"I saw him."

"Where's he from?"

"I don't know, but far away. He has a full black beard and a pistol with a green and gold handle."

"Did you speak to him?"

"No. Only few can speak with him." The Lion pauses and lights a cigarette. "You know, I farmed with my father before all this. He told me I must fight, and now our fields are untended and our animals are scattered. I must go."

"Can we come with you? To see the man?"

"If you come to fight, yes, but to talk, no. I must move quickly. Bye."

The Lion leans the shovel against the tree. He picks up his Kalashnikov and heads up the graveyard hill and disappears into the tree line.

"Where's he going?"

"I don't know; could be mountains away."

"Should we follow?"

"We weren't invited."

"It's not a tea party, Alija."

"Be patient."

"Let's go see Rolo."

Chapter 4

Rolo is a charm bracelet of surprises.

He's American intelligence. That's not as wincing as it sounds. Rolo slipped into these mountains several months ago to track a "little uprising" that had suddenly turned into a pain in the ass for the White House: bowie knives, bodies in clumps, Yugoslav president Slobodan Milosevic slinking in his villa, Bosnia all over again. What to do? The United Nations squawks and condemns, but the drama of outraged ambassadors turns to empty twitter. The Europeans are nauseatingly eloquent in treaties on human rights yet quickly shift to opaque recitations of moral vigor to avoid specific discussions on dispatching their armies to stop slaughter. Rolo's here to see if the U.S. is going to have to do something about the current — shall we call it, as the Europeans do, *untidiness?* — at the fringe of the continent in a place called Kosovo. It's hypnotic terrain: big mountains, wide streams, and air that hangs, once you get away from the smelters and coal plants, in chilled purity, sort of like

Wyoming. Ninety percent Albanian. Ten percent Serb. Kosovo is one of the few strands left of Yugoslavia, which over a decade has shrunk through war and that wonderful euphemism *ethnic cleansing*. The Albanians want independence, but Milosevic and his Serbs have tanks, bigger guns, and reams of nasty, inspirational folklore so easily perverted by nationalists. It's amazing what rabid and insane devotion can be summoned from verse scratched on parchment from centuries past.

I met Rolo years ago in Sri Lanka as he was about to be beheaded by a gang of teenagers with dangling machetes and painted faces. They thought he was an arms dealer of ill-repute, but I, who had hired the son of the village leader as my guide, happened upon the road where Rolo, hands bounds, kneeling, waited beneath a banyan tree for the flash of sunlight and steel. I wandered over and — never underestimate the vagaries of chance and outrageous circumstance, not to mention the cachet of a village connection — convinced them that Rolo was an ecumenical missionary out to save fallen temples. Muddy and stubbly, with a slightly deranged, far-off gaze, Rolo looked the part. The bare-chested machete boys huddled and then turned and laughed and cut him loose. Rolo and I have been crossing paths ever since. *Crossing paths* is Rolo's phrase; he likes the serendipity of it, and he possesses a begrudging sense of indebtedness that is useful for the likes of me. He loves to go native and is partial to Thucydides and Saint Augustine. The son of a South Boston bus driver, Rolo is built low to the ground and tight. He reminds me of a ball of twine with an attitude. He infiltrates the nastiest places on the globe and sends cables back to the shirts and ties and understated blouses in Washington. Typical. One guy does all the humping so a bunch of pasty faces who have never seen a firefight or counted the dead in the morning can finesse intelligence to fit the prevailing political paradigm. *Paradigm* is a popular word in Washington. It's impenetrable, though. There's no cadence, letters without a soul. I'd choose *pitchfork* over *paradigm*.

Alija and I drive and then walk, following a path that winds like a thread through the underbrush and into a clearing. Two guys with guns appear, and moments later I hear that familiar stuffed-up, smoky, perturbed growl: "It's cool, let 'em come."

Rolo leans against a mud hut, a small fire at his feet.

"I thought you were the pizza guy." He laughs. "We called about three months ago. I guess he couldn't find us."

"I didn't know if I'd find you here, either. I thought maybe you had moved on."

"In a few days there will be a relocation," says Rolo, brushing past me. "Let me say hello to the lovelier among you, Jay."

"Hi, Rolo."

"Alija, you remembered. I am touched. I've sensed for some time your attraction toward me. There's a song-from-the-seventies romance going on between us. I can feel it."

"I don't think so, Rolo. I was barely walking in the seventies."

"A sweet decade. Have a tea."

He lifts a blackened kettle from the fire with his rifle barrel. Rolo travels with three local trackers and bodyguards; reticent and loyal, they move across the land like spirits. A face of stubble, hair in a tangle, Rolo is a secret dirt prince, a cipher with satellite phones and global positioning systems.

"You like this little war, Jay?"

"I don't know where it's headed. Milosevic is shaking the dice. He's got one more roll."

"Seems like it's on half-burner though, doesn't it? The guerrillas don't have the arms yet. The fighting kicked up before the hardware arrived. It's starting to get through, though. A lot of shit moving across the Adriatic at night in rubber speedboats. The guerrillas aren't trained, man. These poor bastards, excuse me, Alija, are fighting in sneakers and sandals. You want to win a war, you gotta have boots."

"Not in Africa."

"There's no winter in Africa, O wise journalist."

"The MUP . . ."

"The MUP just want bodies. They don't care whose body. It's classic. Guys go into the mountains to fight. So the MUP, not trained for guerrilla warfare, go to rebel villages, burn their homes, and rape their women. You gotta make a choice, don't you? Do I stay in the mountains, or come back to protect my village? Either way you're in a predicament."

"We getting involved in this, Rolo?"

"Have some more tea, Jay."

Tiny leaves swirl in my tea. It is the same in so many places. Stories told and stories delayed over tea. Amber, deep brown, sometimes green, I can't remember all the cups and *pialas* of tea I've peered into waiting for answers. Sugared and hot, it is the sustenance through which stories flow, connecting native and foreigner, removing boundaries. Every rebel has his rifle and his pouch of tea. Mint. Bitter. A sprig of herb.

Years ago I fled over the Himalayas in Tibet with Buddhist monks who were escaping Chinese soldiers to get to the Dalai Lama in India. We'd trek at night, our line moving swift and speechless like a snake, over rocks and ice, beneath an arc of stars that seemed close enough to swallow. Just before dawn, when yellow and blue splintered a purple horizon, we'd find a crevice to hide in and the monks would build a fire under a blanket and a kettle would appear and tea would be poured as the monks, robed fugitives with frostbitten faces and blistered feet, chanted and sipped before they slept on the gray-brown husk of the world. One of the monks, a raisin-skinned man carrying ancient scrolls, fell ill with fever midway through the two-week journey. His feet tightened, knotted, and balled up; he vomited tea and blood and couldn't go on. The stronger monks huddled in diminutive whispering shadows under the moon. They decided to leave the old monk behind. He would be reincarnated. His soul would be born into a higher life and move a realm closer to the deities sprinkled across the infinite. They explained it to him; he accepted his fate, closing himself into a chant. Back then there was a bit of an altar boy in me. I believed I could save such crumpled characters, either by word or deed. I volunteered to carry him. They looked at one another, then they looked at me, this strange guy with a pencil and dressed in insulated boots and ruffles of Gore-Tex. They protested but then agreed.

I lightened my backpack and folded the monk over my shoulder. I carried him through the night, his chanting body vibrating against mine like the ping of a tuning fork. As we climbed, the oxygen thinned and the monk, light as balsa at eighteen thousand feet, seemed heavy as a car at twenty thousand. I laid him on a rock in a mountain pass. He curled up. I waited and tried to lift him again, but I couldn't. I drank some water, waited, and tried again. I couldn't. Another monk wrapped him in a blanket, and another handed him beads and an empty teacup. They tied a prayer flag to a stick and stuck it in the dirt. We left him. I kept looking back until his gnomic silhouette grew fuzzy and turned to darkness. The monks told me the snows would come and cover the old man until spring, when shepherds would gather him from the thaw and, depending on their religious fervor, would either burn him or cut him into pieces and feed him to birds. Rolo would have appreciated the monks. But guerrillas are on his mind. He rolls a cigarette and leans back, picking dried hay from the mud wall.

"It's getting near dark, Jay."

"Can we stay?"

"You know I don't like that shit. This is Special Ops, man. I'm secret, undercover."

"Just the night. Then we'll be gone. We can't make it back to Pristina by dark, and I don't want to be robbed or ambushed."

"I couldn't very well turn Alija away. Your sorry ass I wouldn't care about."

"Hey, man . . ."

"I know what you're going to ask, Jay. He's here. But we don't know who he is or where he came from. He seemed to appear out of the ether. We don't know why he's here or what he wants."

"I heard this story about dates and donkeys."

"That's the tall tale. Who knows? This guy could be some bad electricity. You remember when the mujahideen enlisted in the Bosnian war, bringing all that Islamic radical shit from Saudi Arabia and the U.A.E. This is like that, but this guy's different. It's like he's some kind of prophet. Some oracle or vision out of Homer. We just don't know, Jay. Be careful if you go hunting him."

Rolo's guys kill a sheep and we eat well. Rolo breathes in the big, clean air, and, sitting around the fire, flames lightening and shadowing his face, he seems a sage, a curious creature folded into a mission that doesn't officially exist in any Washington file. He is what my mother used to call a saint without a heaven. Rolo once told me that his dream was to be a beekeeper: to build wooden hives at the edge of his lawn and sit on his back porch listening to a lulling hum of incessant energy. He said one has to move slowly around bees and that a beekeeper has a monastic quality that Rolo finds intriguing. Alija likes Rolo, though not in the way Rolo likes Alija. She knows that as long as Rolo stays in the mountains other hands are at work, that it isn't just the MUP and the guerrillas, that the landscape has become a kind of big-budget movie with tailored men offstage speaking in euphemisms and cryptic lines about fate and the messiness of realignment.

Alija wants the war to grow. She wants everyone sucked in. She is young, but she is clever enough to know that in the end you need shock and horror, brand-name journalists and TV crews, a smattering of atrocities, outraged congressmen, human-rights lawyers, White House indignation, and just the right number in the Gallup polls, and then, ipso facto, abracadabra, and presto, you've got a full-scale "conflict" with million-dollar bombs. A prime-time, cruise-missile extravaganza. It's the sweepstakes, man. Not everyone wins. Tibet's not going to win. Africa is not even entered, no matter how many dead it can stack up over a weekend. Going to war is like buying a house. Location. Location. Location. The rim of Europe is ideal geography for a fire storm. Alija sleeps with such dreams. Rolo rolls cigarette after cigarette and sits in the light of a dying fire with three men watching his back and the green light flashing on his satellite phone.

I think of cathedrals. Stained glass and candle drip, the shoe scrape, the cool, hewn stone of faith rising into gargoyles and steeples, rising above rivers and rooftops, a place of devotion and commerce, where rosaries and trinkets are sold by Africans waving translucent palms and penance is whispered and redemption granted in a light of burgundy and magenta. Three Hail Marys and two Our Fathers cleanse a soul.

The morning before I returned to this war, I met a whore in a cathedral in Prague. She slipped out of the rain and sat two pews ahead of me, her hair dripping on the wood. Her stockings and her dress gave her away. We were the only two in the church; our pews creaked like ice breaking across a lake. Czechs have been torn on religion since the medieval days, when the Catholics burned reformists at the stake over a theological difference about offering wine at Communion. The Catholics were opposed to it then, and the tussle that ensued divided everything, including the cemeteries, where today Catholic gravestones are marked with the cross while those of Protestants are etched with the chalice. We are inspired and destroyed by symbols. I enjoy sitting amid the centuries-old aftermath of such fury. Battlefields and churches possess the hushed aura of re-invented glories I somehow find soothing. I've visited hundreds of churches across Europe, mostly at dusk when blackened walls make bright the wings of angels. The whore genuflected. She turned and stopped at my pew.

"Do you speak Russian?" she said in English.

"No. English. Italian."

"I want to hear Russian, my language."

"This is a former Soviet country. I'm sure a lot of old Czechs speak Russian."

"Yes, but they want to forget it."

"I can understand that."

"American, right?"

"Yes."

There was a pause. Americans mean recalculation. Not only financial, but cultural. Whores, bartenders, and waiters know this. She was tall, long black hair and blue eyes. The lines of her body were mathematical; Helmut Newton would have loved her, would have posed her in some faded hotel room or on some crooked street; she could have been a leggy mannequin in his grainy fog.

"Listen to the roof. The rain has stopped. Quiet as a prayer. My mom used to say that. Do you live here?"

"No. Traveling."

"Just a traveler, huh? I am traveling, too, but I seem to be suddenly stuck."

"Where are you headed?"

"I don't know. I'm here for a while."

Another pause. She sensed no sale amid the icons and holy water.

"I must go shopping."

"Good-bye."

"Tomorrow I am working, maybe you can call me. I know how to please American men."

She handed me a card, one like thousands of others sprinkled across the cobblestones and stuffed onto windshields. So much glamour on those little cards, promises attached to telephone numbers of girls far from their native tongues. Her card showed a champagne glass with a topless woman — not her — sitting cross-legged and bending down as if to tell a secret from the hood of a Mercedes on a dark street. Prague? Budapest? Berlin?

"I'm leaving tomorrow."

"Maybe another time. Learn Russian and come back."

She laughed, clicked over the stones, and stepped through the big wooden door into the gray light. I'll think of her for a long time. An encounter so brief there is no chance for it to be spoiled, sweetly preserved for its lack of progression. Rolo kicks me awake.

"Jay. Jay."

"What?"

"Me and the boys are splitting, breaking camp."

"Now?"

"Dark is best."

"You'll contact me the same way?"

"Yeah, don't worry, we'll meet again."

"Hey, Rolo. I want the bearded guy with the dates."

"He's got quite the dance card, that guy."

"Dance card, Jesus, Rolo. You have to watch some movies made this century."

"I don't know if he's a guy we want around, you know?"

"What are you saying?"

"I'm saying I'm breaking camp. Bye, Jay."

He and his men roll quietly away. Alija sleeps. I take my blanket and lie next to her in the broken house. Who lived here before the war? Where have they gone? Strangers sleep in their rooms. A few belongings left behind. An old shoe, a dish towel, grains of rice, a cup. Unseen spirits and the artifacts of wrecked lives, moving somewhere, shifting, but where, where do they go? The hills? The mountains? Scattered with children, schools in the rain, hauling river water, campfires and morning ash. Hiding. The Lion digs a grave; a wheat field shrivels. Sometimes I think I'd like to gather the children and calm the fields, but I cannot. I have come poorly armed, a man of paper and ink in a land of blood and war. I am a curiosity to them, recording and cataloguing like a requisition agent or a government clerk. Nothing changes when the words dry. If you cannot heal a wound, extract a bullet, or kill the enemy, why have you come? This is what's in their eyes when I uncap my pen and turn to a blank page in my notebook.

A cool wire runs through the night. Dawn is a few hours away. I turn toward Alija. I remember when we met. Scared and angry in that camp, she carried, as she does now, secrets and shame even in sleep.

35

Chapter 5

Brian Conrad is in his best outraged-journalist mode, yet he's losing the battle to a little man in a polyester suit.

"What do you mean I need a press pass?"

"These are the rules," says the suit.

"This is a guerrilla war, man. There are no rules."

"Still, you need a press pass to travel in our territory."

"You don't have any territory."

"We have checkpoints. We control some roads."

"This is fucking ridiculous."

"There are rules."

"Okay, okay. Where do I get the press pass?"

"The man who gives them is not here."

"Where is he?"

"I don't know. Come back tomorrow."

"But I need to travel in the mountains today."

"There are rules. He'll be here tomorrow. Maybe, while you wait, you can do a story on one of our woman fighters.

We can provide her today. We have a number of women fighters. Our struggle is big."

"I don't want to interview a woman fighter. Women fighters aren't news anymore. Women are fighting all over the fucking place."

"*Fuck* is an important word for you. Can you write this word in American newspaper?"

Brian would beg if it would do any good, but the guy in the suit is impervious, sitting behind a desk with pens all in a row. There's a final verbal torrent and a furious burst of hand gestures, then Brian plunks in a chair, defeated. He doesn't notice that Alija and I have been standing behind him.

"Getting your ass kicked?"

"Jay, don't mess with me."

"Guy's not going to budge, is he?"

"Well, my friend, it's like this. Communist bureaucracy dies hard even for the rebels. Seems we now need press passes. These guys want to overthrow the government but keep the system. Rubber stamps and paperwork. Something to busy these guys while the MUP kicks their asses. Guerrilla press passes. What's going on in the world, Jay?"

"We don't charge you for the press pass," the man chirps happily.

"Small favors," snaps Brian. "This guy says without a press pass we can't cross rebel checkpoints."

"What do you think?"

"I think I need a beer."

"A fucking beer." The man smiles. "Don't worry,

mister. Tomorrow we will get you a press pass. Remember the woman fighter."

The village is dusty, a guerrilla outpost tucked in a mountain crease. Smuggled weapons are sold, money is exchanged from car trunks, bread and meat are ferried in, a barber cuts hair on a porch, rebel commanders whisk by in Kia SUVs, and young men, who weeks ago were working as diaspora waiters in Belgium and Switzerland, linger in the shade in shiny, mismatching fatigues. They come in scattered legions, bouncing across the Adriatic on rubber boats to join their brothers and fathers, their bravado pierced by the wandering eye of an old guy sitting on a rock and writing wills while hunched over a briefcase. Traffic is heavier than it was when I came through ten days ago. The place has the feel and energy of a poor man's boot camp lorded over by men with grenades hanging like fruit from their vests.

"Well, Jay, we're going down the rabbit hole."

"Seems so."

"Build an army. Men with guns. Assembly required."

"How much training you think these guys get?"

"Training? Give me a break. They get, 'Here's your AK. Follow that path into the woods and kill somebody.'"

"Ye of little faith, Brian."

"Jay, I don't want a full-scale war at this particular moment. I have three weeks' vacation coming. Fiji. After that, fine."

"Let's go see who's in charge."

"That house, there. It's the only one without a mortar hole."

The Leopard has the finest mustache in the Balkans. It is the first thing you notice. The gentle conceit of a refined man caught in unexpected circumstances. He waves his two sentries away and rises to greet us. Tea appears before we sit. Brian, in his usual manner, plunks in a chair, crosses his legs, and eases into a cynical slouch, biting on his pen, tightening his eyes. The Leopard folds his tapered hands. Alija sits at the desk next to him.

"Thank you for coming," says the Leopard through Alija.

"Things seem to be happening."

"They are. Weather dictates much. Winter is not far away."

"And money?" says Brian.

The Leopard doesn't respond and eases to another tack.

"We are tired of the way we live. We are changing that."

"Do you have enough firepower?" says Brian, pushing for more.

"Not yet, but it's coming. The MUP are one-speed. They know how to surround and shell villages. But they don't know how to fight an enemy on the move. We will be mercurial."

"Alija," says Brian. "Is *mercurial* the accurate translation?"

Before she answers, the Leopard says, "Yes." He shifts to English.

"In my previous life, the one I had until five months ago, I was a human-rights lawyer in Pristina. But the MUP doesn't pay attention to human rights. I was tired of filing petitions, tired of losing young men in places I could never again find them. I'm a commander here because I'm educated. I've never killed a man. But I think I can now. I will."

"I hear you have mercenaries from the West training some of your fighters. I've seen some Chevy Suburbans with the tinted glass roaming around up here. We know who drives those."

The Leopard purses his lips, his mustache falling like a curtain.

"When were you last attacked here?"

"A few days ago, the MUP came. We fought only a few hours and retreated to the hills."

"This is not your headquarters?"

"No, this is the lowest territory we hold. Our strong places are in the mountains."

"How many men have you lost?"

The Leopard does not respond.

"How many fighters do you have?"

Silence.

"Who's your top commander?"

Nothing.

"Any talks with the MUP or negotiations going on?"

"No."

"Do we really need a press pass to go into the mountains?" says Brian.

The Leopard laughs.

"So, you've run into our office of registration. That's Mr. Hani. A civil servant in another life. A meticulous man. You probably don't need a press pass, but why not humor him. It would be better to have it than not. You can stay the night here. If the MUP come, though, you're on your own." The Leopard stands, smoothes his mustache.

"Do you all have animal noms de guerre?" I say.

He laughs again. "Yes, we have many Lions and Leopards and Panthers. Not many Elephants or Ducks. We do have a Salamander."

"I'd like to meet him." Brian flashes a half-smirk, one of a dozen or so facial variations in his interview repertoire.

The Leopard disappears out the door with his sentries.

"I was serious," Brian says to Alija. "I want to meet the Salamander. He's got to be original. I bet he's the best fucking interview up here."

"You know, you ought to curb the *fuck*. These guys are Muslims."

"They have a song now," he says, looking to me. "Have you heard it? Some guerrilla's daughter recorded it in Tirana. A real heartstring tugger. Heavy percussion, rising chorus, lots of references to blood and land and bravery. A freedom song, man. It's officially here, Jay, a ditty for a war coming to a theater near you."

"You're kidding, right?"

"I'm not. I told you we're going down the rabbit hole."

"You think the mujahideen is coming? That would raise the level of play."

"They're here, man. We just can't see 'em."

"I don't think these guys will buy the muj."

"We'll see."

Brian and I have reached that journalistic juncture between competition and camaraderie. I don't think he knows about the dateman, but I hadn't seen the Chevy Suburbans or heard that crazy song he's talking about. Suburbans mean the spooks are here, not Rolo's tribe but most likely State Department ops accompanying a diplomatic envoy. Washington's trying to contain this thing. They're reaching out to the guerrillas. Washington wants the MUP gone, but the guerrillas, as I am witnessing, are an unknown quantity, driven by what and run by whom?

I'd rather be on my own with this. But Brian's a good man, and he's here and it's safer traveling in twos. Which means I have to share the dateman. That prospect is not bothering me like it would have fifteen years ago. Then, I would have wanted the exclusive. But we change, don't we? You want to scoop some guy at city hall or in Washington, that's fine. But here the land explodes, houses burn, women are sliced and raped, dirt paths vanish into thickets, road-blocks appear like gangster lemonade stands armed with drunken MUP or jittery guerrillas. You can get lost in this, get lost and never get out. No story. No exclusive. You end up a cautionary tale around the hack bar at night; you become that moment of silence, a scribe briefly remembered between sips of whiskey and speculation about who is going to bed whom in the hours after deadline. I scraped one colleague off a road years ago somewhere in the sub-Sahara. I slipped him into my trunk and drove him seventy miles to an airfield with a dirt runway and paid a diamond/arms smuggler five hundred dollars to fly me and the body to some sliver of civilization, where I found a consulate and two guys brought a rubber bag with a zipper and I signed some forms, went back to the diamond/arms smuggler, paid another five hundred dollars to fly back into the jungle, and before dusk filed a story about a massacre of refugees. The story landed on page A-10, behind a piece on the dangers of cosmetic surgery and some badly written tale about cod fishing. These days I wince when I hear an editor or some media bean counter talk about commitment to journalism. It did exist once, beautiful, untrammeled. But now that commitment begins only after the shareholders get their 21 percent and incompetent CEOs wheedle the legalese of golden parachutes. Let 'em have it. All I want is the quiet, lingering mystery in the stories of the day.

"Hey, Alija. What do you think about Brian traveling with us?"

"We'll never get sleep. That guy's always on. And he borrows stuff."

"Yeah, but it might be safer with an extra body. It won't be constant. It'll be off and on. He'll peel away and do his own stuff sometimes."

"He doesn't even have a translator."

"That's where you come in."

"Oooh, a verbal threesome. How perverse."

"It's your call."

"Fine. I just want to find my brother, Jay. We'll get your stories. We'll get the dateman, but I have to keep looking for my brother."

So we are three, all imbued with and moved by different rhythms. We eat bread and cheese and listen to the rattle and packing of young fighters preparing to leave camp. The Leopard summons us at night. He has four men with him, and he leads us out of the village and onto an ascending path. Clouds are ghosting the moon, and the breeze chills the sweat on my brow as we crest a ridge and walk the midsection of a mountain. No one speaks; we are a discordant chorus of breaths, and sometimes a kicked rock clatters and our breathing stops as the Leopard holds up his hand and listens. I think about mines and tracer fire, whores and cathedrals. The Leopard leads us down. We trace a stream, and the land softens.

"I didn't sign up for this," says Brian.

"Quiet, man."

"Shit, Jay, I hated the Boy Scouts."

Brian laughs. Hating something only makes him happier. The Leopard stops us before a clearing. He hands me binoculars. They are night-vision, not the toy of your everyday rebel. A MUP checkpoint lies two hundred meters south. Two armored personnel carriers and about twenty soldiers, their cigarette embers moving like lazy fireflies.

"We're going to attack," says the Leopard.

"What?"

"Not us. Our men over there. We watch from here."

"What time is it, Jay?"

"Two a.m."

"Shit, we're going to miss deadline."

"Quiet," says Alija.

A click and a whoosh. Two mortars explode near the checkpoint. Kalashnikovs flash as the guerrillas advance, a team from the north and another from the east. A rocket-

44

propelled grenade whistles and strikes one of the armored personnel carriers, exploding like a flower blooming against velvet. The MUP scatter. The other APC snaps to life, its headlights cutting out over the fields, illuminating haystacks. Radios crackle. The MUP return fire with a .50-caliber machine gun humming from a trench. Dogs howl, and the MUP are yelling and cursing and suddenly the crazy bullet barrage stops and the guerrillas recede like a wave, falling back into the darkness as smoke obscures the checkpoint and a thread of fire burning leaking APC fuel squiggles down the dirt road. The MUP chase the guerrillas heading east but can't cut them off before the guerrillas vanish into the forest cover. The MUP don't want to go there, and they spin and head back to the checkpoint. We run along the stream and climb, skirting the mountain ridge, silhouetted in the blue-gray light of the moon. It starts to drizzle, and the land gets slippery. Alija nearly tumbles and the Leopard grabs her arm, hurrying her around the bend and into rebel territory, where he and his men smile at their victory. The Leopard speaks into his radio. Five dead MUP, three dead guerrillas, one battered APC. We return to the village. The Leopard disappears.

"That was beautiful," says Alija.

"A pinprick," says Brian.

"You don't get it. My people never had the will to do this before. We kept choking on peaceful resistance — Gandhi translated into our tongue. But the words might as well have been spoken underwater. Nothing happened. Tonight I saw MUP scared. I've never seen that before. Do you understand what that's like?"

"Okay," says Brian. "But you know what will happen next. Tomorrow, or the next day, the MUP will retaliate and burn a village. Until the Leopard and his crew can hold the bottomland and take some cities, raids like tonight's are illusions."

"It's still sweet."

Brian is right. So is Alija. It's nearly dawn. Breakfast fires flicker as I close my eyes. The Leopard is another man I need to know better.

Chapter 6

War is a peacock with many feathers. Let us meet some MUP. We leave the Leopard's village and drive west, past the ambushed MUP checkpoint. The APC smolders in the rain. Bullet casings sparkle like scattered pennies in the dirt. The MUP are busy reestablishing. Uncoiling razor wire and fortifying bunkers, they wave us on without hassle. Advance to Go. A wonderful feeling. Brian's sleeping in the back, and Alija, as she does whenever we cross into MUP real estate, puts on her mask face, pale and tight as a drum skin. Religion changes the patina of the land; village mosques turn to village churches. Allah versus Saint George slaying the dragon. Koran passages, Orthodox epic poems, and old battlefields blur mind and rainy windshield. Around a bend, then another, past a cemetery to a house by a water mill, where Milan Babic's family has been grinding wheat into bread for three hundred years. The Jeep crackles over the loose stones in the driveway. The house door opens and out comes Milan, a big man in a gray zip-up MUP suit with a 9mm holstered at his side and a bowie knife slipped into his boot. Green eyes dipped in hazel, Milan could love you or kill you, depending on the instant.

"How are you, Jay? I haven't seen you in months, at least."

"I took some time off."

"Let's have coffee. You must be tired of drinking Muslim tea."

I step toward him, my hand lost in his big one, his arm heavy on my shoulder.

"Smoke?"

"Quit."

"Jesus, Jay. Don't get American on me. Believe me, before this is all over, you'll be smoking again."

I let Brian sleep in the Jeep. Alija keeps her mask on and stays there too. Milan and I walk into the water mill. Stone walls and mud held together for centuries. Drying peppers hang from wooden beams near a painting of Prince Lazar, the Serb hero whose legions were destroyed by the Ottoman Turks in the 1300s in a battle not far from here. They call it the Field of Blackbirds. The Serbs have long felt misunderstood; they are Europe's brooding half-cousin, and their bitterness flows from the graves of Lazar's army.

Milan's waterwheel creaks and shimmies. The stone gully that carries the water away has been smoothed by time, like the steps of an Italian church, shiny and worn, the color of butterscotch and ivory. Milan sits at a wooden table with a map and lights a few candles. He pours two coffees and two plum brandies and motions for me to sit. He spreads the map in front of me. Here is land in miniature, the heights of mountains, bent streams, roads, farm fields, cities, village specks, and red circles.

"Those are the guerrilla positions. All in the mountains. They don't hold them for long. They're seeds in the wind, Jay. One place then another."

"You guys aren't good at mountain fighting."

"We wait them out. They can have the mountains and the birds. We have the cities and the villages." He stops, agitated. "I don't get it. America is supporting Muslims against Christians. This is Europe, man. The Christians and the Americans should stick together, or we'll all be bending over for the call to prayer."

It isn't time to discuss the finer points of how MUP brutality, a decade of repression, and mass graves got us here. There are few places in the world so skilled at historical revision. Whatever happened when it happened is never as it happened. Milan goes on for a while and then quiets. You have to let the Serbs prattle for a bit, travel through the centuries, and then they settle down and you can speak to them of modern things.

"I've been fighting eight years. Croatia, Vukovar. Sarajevo. Here. It's like they keep making new games of war, widening the board, adding a few more pieces and reselling it."

"Your board's shrinking, Milan."

"We're tap dancing on the edge."

He walks to the corner and pulls a tarp off an upright piano. He blows off dust and sits on a stool.

"It's damp in here, but it's kept a little of its tone."

His hands lift toward the keys. They hover, not unsure

49

but contemplating, and then a single note shimmers, and then another and a third and then a riffle at the tinkling end of the register, and then he lulls it back to the deep keys, where he holds it like a voice. I have heard him play several times, a jazzman following the resonant, circuitous lines of Art Tatum and Bill Evans, his fingers moving in the broken light and shadow of the millstone. His hands are smooth, almost sanded; they don't fit the rest of him. His father was a classical pianist when Yugoslavia was still whole. The old man taught Milan jazz from LPs smuggled in from Montenegro. Then he disappeared. The euphemism for a nation: *disappear.* As if one day he'll reappear with a stack of records under his arm and new songs to teach his son. War has kept Milan from opening the club he wants, a little place, he says, with cheap drinks and the kind of curtains they had in the 1940s, that thick red material tipped with gold, smoky tassels. Not here but somewhere else in Europe. He misses a note and unholsters his 9mm and pretends to shoot the piano. He goes back to the orphan note and finds it, holding it longer than he should, then releasing it and backtracking to it and playing around it and going to it again, until the note finally obeys, lingering for a moment and then slipping mute beneath the keys.

"Remember Sarajevo?"

"I was heading out with my artillery unit. You journalists were all over the place."

"Bees. We're like bees."

"Bees on windows. Drink your coffee, Jay."

Milan was a man-boy in Sarajevo. There were many of them back then. Ripped fatigues and scared, mean faces.

Milan shelled the city in six-hour shifts, and toward the end they trained him to be a sniper. He could kill Muslim women and old men at five hundred meters. They thought they were protected, clinging to walls, tiptoeing around corners, creeping like stealthy cats. They were stick people in his scope. Their blood spilled on tram tracks, sidewalks, riverbanks, and courtyards. Sarajevo was blood and vegetables and cobblestones, and sometimes the blood made shapes — a tree, a car, a face — the way clouds make shapes in the sky. A sniper's scope exposes all. You look the fool before a death you don't see or hear coming. Bullet travels distance, compresses time. You fall. No one runs to help. You are in the sights. You are marked. Your groceries and firewood scattered. When the sniper sleeps, your family comes and pulls you quickly away in the darkness, a smear in the moonlight following you home.

When I met him Milan sat alone atop an APC. His unit was preparing to pull back, and Milan was thumbing a tiny notebook, his ledger of death. Each kill recorded: time, date, wind condition, snow or rain. No names. Who were they? They were movements, he said. Twitches in a street, a streak of color at a corner. You're young, I said. I killed seventy-three people, how can I be young? he answered. He and his unit retreated into the sleet and ice. A year later, I was in a Belgrade psychiatric hospital doing a piece on the trauma of war. An editor-assigned story; I hate it when they think big and abstract. But there was Milan, sitting knotlike in a chair, looking out a window. The drawn boy from Sarajevo had grown beefy and stubble-faced. He held his death ledger. He half remembered me. The doctor said Milan would sometimes stand at the window and pretend he was a sniper again. Other times he would cry. He once tried to jump off the roof. He said he wanted to fly, but the doctor told him he'd left his wings in his room and he should try another day. I visited him a few times. We sat mostly in silence. Men stumbled between piss and shit, reality and glorious invention, shuffling on floors in plastic sandals. One told me his daughter was living on the moon. He sent her there before his village was stormed. "She watches me from her high window in the sky," he said. "She will come soon. She'll follow the starlight to me and take me away. There are men here trying to kill me. Special agents. Men with many faces and disguises. They know what I have seen."

I gave Milan my card before I left Belgrade. He slipped it into his notebook and said he'd call. You know, he said, perching in the window twilight, I never fired a headshot. The other guys used to aim for the heads, but I never did. I couldn't. Why is that? Maybe, he said, he didn't really want to kill them. He just wanted to knock them down. "They were Muslims, screw 'em, but maybe it's good from a human point of view that I didn't go for the head. What do you think?" I don't remember what I answered. What could I say? Sure, Milan, shooting someone through the heart is much less insane. I left him with his riddle. I received a letter from him years later. "I'm better," he wrote. "Rationalization doesn't work. I did what I did. I'm not asking forgiveness. Who would grant it anyway? I've been made a lieutenant and have been reassigned to my family home in Kosovo." So wonderfully, typically Serb.

"Milan, who's leading the guerrillas?"

"Some locals and a few outsiders. The money is coming from the diaspora in Switzerland and Austria. A little drug cash from Italy, but not much of that. This is Yugoslavia's unfinished chapter, Jay. Macedonia is its own country. Croatia, Slovenia, Bosnia. All broken away from the great Serb dream. And, now, Kosovo."

"I heard they have this bearded guy who came across the mountains on horseback or on a donkey or something?"

"Heard of him. Haven't seen him."

"Think he's for real?"

"It's the Balkans, Jay, who knows. But, yeah, he probably is. The Muslims want this land just like they did five hundred years ago. Pretty soon they're gonna want your country. The eternal struggle, huh? Been going on since before the Crusades."

"A philosopher and a historian."

"Just a sniper."

Milan pours another brandy. He takes his glass and rises from the piano. I follow him into the rain. We walk across his yard, past his plum and apple trees and into the field toward the village church. Mist hangs like angel hair in the wheat. The horizon is gray and stunted and I think of being lost out here, wandering in the rain between fields and tree lines, following a stream and wondering whose army would find me first, who would kill me based upon the arrangement of vowels and consonants in my last name. The rain falls heavy, rattling all around but calm. Blackbirds caw and preen in trees. Milan and I stop at the cemetery. Weeds and a rusted fence. The gravestones are slick with chiseled faces of the dead. Most of the markers are gray and white. Milan stops in front of a black one.

"Why are some black, Jay?"

"I don't know."

"If you write about this land you should know."

"Tell me."

"The black stone marks the man who sold his land to a Muslim. He is shamed forever."

Chapter 7

Alija's mask softens as we cross the last MUP checkpoint. We're back on her land, out of range, at least for now, from Milan's sniper scope. Her brother is lucky. If I were lost, I would like to have Alija worrying and searching for me, going from village to village, her questions direct, her demeanor pulling close whomever is listening, her fingers dusted and sticky with the gumdrop sugar that collects in the deep pockets of her coat. Where are you, Ardian? Who are you? A young man, a boy, really, a student, lost. Alija protected you from the Serb boys when you were young; she says you were slight and scared most of the time, but then there was that day when the Serb called you a name and you fought at the edge of a field, hoping your father would come, but he didn't and you had to finish on your own, walking home bloody, your shirt torn. Alija likes that story. It is the only fighter story she tells about you. She says your English is as fine as hers and that your favorite possession is a silver cigarette case you bought in a Macedonian market. You like how thin and delicate it is, the way it rides in your shirt pocket. You pull it out to impress the girls; Alija says the girls like you even without the case, but like many boys you don't see this. She says you are good with computers and that sometimes you take them apart and run your fingers over their circuitry. She has a picture of you two. You're both running. The sun must be in front of you; your face is clear, russet, the face of a boy chasing his sister home.

The MUP fade in the rearview, and a tinny call to prayer warbles from a loudspeaker in a minaret. Nobody bends to pray. The poor, the farmers, and the village boys are in motion. Cattle trundle to pasture, the sheep graze in the highlands. The rain stops and the sun breaks; the mud roads spatter. Brian awakens and wants to fish.

"I've got a story to file."

"It's early. We can write later. Let's catch some dinner."

Alija rolls her eyes.

I had forgotten that Brian, no matter how hostile the terrain, travels with a collapsible fishing pole, lures, hooks, and a rumpled straw hat his father or some ancient uncle must have given him when he was a kid. He has fished rivers in war zones across the world. He is slow and methodical. The din of battle does not deter him. He ties flies and studies the flow and swirl of rivers. I like this about him. He has another life, splintered passions that move him beyond the news and set him, it seems to me, in a private, yet oddly kinetic, solitude. The energy fits his frame, tall but not spindly, with a bit of wire and muscle around the shoulders and neck as if he does push-ups when no one is watching. His hair is long, with a slight black curl, and wild, flowing around a face with brown eyes teetering on cheekbones more rounded than finely edged.

He sometimes appears larger than he is, his personality and the robust whine of his voice moving ahead of him the way clouds foretell a summer storm. There's journalist folklore that Brian was once fishing a river in Chechnya near where separatists were sneaking along the shoals ahead of an advancing Russian army. The rebels stopped, perplexed over this lanky foreigner standing knee-deep in the cold water, flicking his wrist as filament whirred and danced across the surface. They mimicked him, and, despite being chased by Russians, the Chechens, a tempestuous people with a taste for fun and a penchant for brutality, decided to show Brian how one fishes in the Caucasus. A grenade plunked. The rebels dove into the underbrush; Brian scurried for shore. Dead fish rose like blossoming flowers. The forest rumbled with laughter as the Chechens disappeared, a swift retreating tribe of tinkling metal. The Russians arrived seconds later and debated shooting Brian. But he waded back into the river, collected the fish, and invited them to dinner. They ate and drank bottles of vodka, and Brian traveled with the Russians for three days until they got to Grozny and the fighting got heavy and they told Brian he was on his own.

"Alija," he says, "I need a river with rocks and a touch of white water. Not too fast, not too slow, a place where the water is cool and clean and moving. Where can we go?"

"There's a bend by an old Roman bridge about thirty minutes from here. We have to park and walk."

"Let's go. See that, Jay? We're gonna fish by a Roman bridge. Last night, we saw an ambush, and today we're fishing by a Roman bridge. What more could you want?"

"What would your editor say?"

"Jay, I'm convinced my editor doesn't read. He's oblivious. Doesn't know a thing about the world, just wants to have his morning budget filled so he can carry a doughnut and a coffee into a meeting and pretend that he's got a handle on all the little windstorms out there. Let's not spoil this lovely day with talk of editors."

"This is it, Brian. We're not going to be fishing all over the Balkans."

"You won't miss anything by a little bit of reeling and casting. You know the saying, God doesn't hold against a man the time a man spends fishing."

The stone architecture of the small Roman bridge is perfect. It's a thing worthy of study and admiration, but its hewed angles and simple majesty will be overlooked, if not bombed, in the present chaos. Empires bursting forth and then receding, bones and bridges and spearheads left behind in an incomplete puzzle. This is the world. Brian unzips his bag and grabs his gear. Alija leads us under the bridge and into the trees that trace the river. The water clears, and stones arch out of the current.

"Perfect, Alija, just perfect."

Brian clicks and unfolds things, ties a lure, and splashes into the river. Arm swaying, he settles into a rhythm, his line rolling out over the water like a thin, lazy snake. There's purity to the curls and loops, each one never to be recreated in an amalgam of mathematics, human imprecision, and art conspiring gently in the sunlight beyond the trees.

Alija and I sit on the bank and watch.

So many months ago we met. The clashes had just started. Hers was one of the first villages burned. Three of her cousins were killed, and she and her mother and father ended up in a tent at a Red Cross camp. Her brother had already disappeared, and she suspected he may have enlisted with the guerrillas. I arrived in the camp with another translator. Men played backgammon on a box, and one of them, Alija's father, invited us for tea. He was small, a flyweight with thick brown hands and a belt yanked to the last notch. He wore a vest and a pinstriped blazer, a rich man's coat donated and handed down the line until the day he must have plucked it from a donkey cart at Saturday market. How many borders crossed and how many miles had that coat traveled? How many peasants slipped their arms through its sleeves? A few buttons missing. An archipelago of faded stains. A rip that could be mended and, inside, the glow of silk lining, dirty and tattered but still smooth, even a bit glossy in places, that suggested something regal with a fine name embroidered over the pocket. He opened the coat and pointed.

"Lon-don."

He smiled and pulled back the tent flap. Alija was sitting on a cot in a corner. Unlike most young Muslim women, she did not turn away when I looked at her. A row of stitches, black and spindly like an insect, ran under her left eye. Her bruises were yellow and plum. Vaseline was smeared over the scabbed nicks on her face. She seemed to glisten in the half-light as her father and mother lifted a teakettle and cups and told us to sit. Her father smiled. Her mother offered sugar. Our tiny spoons stirred and clinked as if we were a chamber orchestra tuning up for an afternoon performance. The canvas scent of the tent was strong in the heat, and the dust in the still air did not float so much as hover. I looked to my translator and prepared to start my litany of questions: name, age, village, how many relatives, all the incidentals that relax someone before you get to the real stuff.

"I will translate for my family," Alija said.

There was no lilt, no hesitation. How does one possess such a clear voice? No fragments of inhibition. Not hard or threatening, but direct, as if soul, heart, and mind moved like animals in unison. I liked its pitch. The way it sought to protect and control. I thought of a singer's voice at the end of a night, a bit raspy, but hiding in it somewhere a strength that could rise when summoned. She stepped off the cot and pointed to bags of rice and flour. Like her father's coat, they bore names from respectable places. She looked at them.

"This is what you get when they burn your house down. I thought somehow you'd get more."

"Where did you learn English?"

"He said to the heathen. School and movies. When I was a girl, the UN sent a couple of aid workers to our village. They mostly worked with the farmers. One of them was an Australian woman. She taught me English and read to me every day for two years. I may be the only one in these mountains who can tell you what happened to Pip and Miss Haversham."

"How long have you been in this camp?"

She sat between her parents. Her father leaned slightly away. It seemed an unconscious tilt, as if some unfinished domestic skirmish had traveled with them from their previous life. War drains and preoccupies, but it does not extinguish. Family battles go on violently, imperceptibly, like ice cubes frozen over time at different temperatures. The curse of war is not dying; it's living through the mess with all the unresolved things that were there long before the first shot was fired. Alija's mother held her daughter's hand and stroked her hair, balancing the slight space left by her father. Alija's face stayed cut and unreadable.

"I can work for you," she said.

"He has a translator," said my translator.

"I know what you do."

"You know nothing."

"I've seen you in the villages. You spy for the MUP."

She turned to me.

"You should be more careful."

My translator rushed toward Alija. From the inner pocket that said Lon-don, Alija's father drew a pistol. My translator stopped. The barrel was point blank, but the old man was shaking and I noticed for the first time the bright blue slivers of his eyes. He clicked a round into the chamber. My translator leaned back and spoke to Alija in their native tongue. Alija's father interjected twice. I didn't understand the words. The translator rose and asked to be paid for the day. His fists were balled, and he was breathing heavily. I wasn't upset about losing him; he was lazy and liked to drink. I paid him and he left, shouting something as he burst through the flap in the tent, a flash of dust, shadow, and sunlight. Alija's father eased the trigger. He was pale. Her mother stopped his shaking hand and slipped the pistol into the silk lining of his coat. The man smiled and sipped his tea as his wife shooed a few flies and offered more sugar from her Red Cross sack.

"So now I can work for you," said Alija.

"What happened?"

"I told you. He spies for the MUP. How long did you use him?"

"A few days. My usual guy quit. Decided he had enough of the fighting and went to Italy. I was trying out new people."

"Everything you did, everyone you saw, the MUP knows now too."

"How do you know?"

"We all know our traitors."

"How do I know you don't work for the MUP?"

"Look at my face."

"I travel all over. What about your parents? I need someone who will stay with me, maybe for months."

"I'm ready. My parents are fine. We can give them some of my pay now."

I handed her five hundred dollars. She kissed her mother and pushed the money into her palm. She said nothing to her father. She snapped back the tent flap, and I followed this bruised-face girl and her wonderful English. She was scared and steely all at the same time. Another morning going one way, then reinvented. Another life slips in, and the syntax and the rhythms change in your notebook. Somebody new is telling you what's true and false, and you have to trust her because language is a weapon in war.

"Look at him," says Alija, pointing to Brian in the river.

"I don't think he's caught anything."

"He won't."

"He might. He's got a lot of hooks and lines."

"The river's dead down here."

"You're kidding. Why did you bring us?"

"To watch him. To see how long he'll stand there jerking his wrist and hoping."

"You're wicked."

"Jay, admit it. He deserves it." She laughs.

"I like Brian."

"I like him enough, but sometimes don't you just want to jab him?"

"Yeah, but I'm wasting hours on a fish I'll never eat while I could be writing."

"You're a fast writer. What's the problem?"

"Age."

"You're not even forty, are you?"

"Not that kind of age. It's details, you know. A lot of the older hacks have lost the sense for detail, the precision of a simple thing. You can read it in their copy. There's stuff missing. They go for big sweeping paragraphs because they don't take the time anymore to collect the miniature. They think they already know it. But the grain changes. You have to see it. I never want to lose the details."

"It's about what you pick. Why one description's chosen over another, right?"

"They must accumulate into something."

"Yes, but you're the collector and the chooser. You get the say. What if you pick the wrong detail?"

"You're careful. You don't rush. Close your eyes and describe my face."

"What?"

"You see it every day. Describe it."

"Come on, Jay."

"Really."

"I'm not good at this. Okay, here goes. Black hair, pins of gray. Strong face but not what it was, I bet. The lines around the eyes . . . oh, what's that word?"

"*Deep. Ravaged.*"

She laughs.

"*Prevalent*, that's it. Prevalent, but soft."

"Like thumbprints?"

"More like spider webs. Nearly invisible."

"What else?"

"Dark, far-back eyes, but not mysterious. Intense, though."

"Intellectual?"

"No, more sexual."

"Thank God."

"The smile evens it out. The spider webs rise on the smile."

"A face of balance?"

"No. It's a face of waiting, I think."

"Waiting. Waiting for what?"

"I don't know. It's a lighted face pressed against the window in the night."

"I think we'll stop at the face. You picked the details. Are they right? Precise enough?"

She opens her eyes and puts a hand on my cheek.

"I don't know, Jay, but it's a good face."

"Why should I believe you? You've got me sitting along a dead river."

"A pretty river with no fish. Sleep with me tonight?"

"Sleeping with you is like being on a river with no fish."

"You don't mind the way we do it?"

"We don't do it."

"But you understand, right? Jay, let me tell you the story tonight."

"Where's it going?"

"You'll see. But it won't finish tonight. It can't."

Brian slogs through the river toward us.

"Any bites?"

"A few. The lures must be wrong."

Alija laughs.

"Looks like sheep again. I'm tired of eating sheep. Alija, you guys gotta get some more animals on this land."

Night. A breeze tugs from the west, and clouds slip across the moon. Voices. The creak of the last donkey cart home. A boy giggles, and the lights go out in this village we have found. Fires in stoves, white smoke curling through the sky. It is a good night, the villagers think. The day has been fine, and the darkness is crisp. The guerrillas are hiding, and MUP will not come tonight. No, they will not come. Even the MUP need rest. Maybe tomorrow they will come. Someone may die tomorrow. But not tonight; there is just the feeling that this night will pass quietly. Men with rifles gather. Their cigarette embers glow. One patrols there, another there. Nothing moving. The roads are still. The fields are quiet. I told you nothing will happen tonight. The children sleep. The wives wait in beds for their men, shadows pulling back covers; skin touches skin and it seems like a moment long ago, before all this, but then a distant sound, just a muffle really, but it hangs out there and the men say, no, no, not tonight, maybe tomorrow but not tonight. Alija forgets to tell me her story, the one of cuts and bruises, the one that never ends. She sleeps on my shoulder. Her body runs alongside mine as if in a Klimt painting; her breasts brush my arm, her belly skims my hip, her feet glide along my calf. Our bodies, two countries, enmeshed, folded, curved at a border of bone and skin. How do you cross such a border and do no harm? Borders are long and there are many places to breach, but where, you wonder where, if at all? Down the hall in this little house we have found for the night, Brian sleeps in a scattered storm of notebooks, papers, maps, and at least one bottle of raki. He is fishless but filed, his story sent across invisible miles to the computer of an editor who doesn't read.

Out the window, beyond the cool fields and checkpoints, where the flatlands begin their ascent, Milan is sleeping too, or maybe he's perched on a ridge and peering through an infrared scope. There is little starlight. Not much to see. But snipers look for shimmers in the terrain, and some can spot a breath when it's not even winter. Rolo, where is he on this night? Camped and in a sleeping bag. A stone hidden in a pocket. So many restless creatures out there. Atoms spinning. And ghosts. Maybe the Romans are crossing the perfect bridge that spans Alija's dead, pretty river. They have their masons and their stone cutters, their generals and their plebes, and they move with the slight clatter of swords and shields, lanterns dangling before them and leading the way. The real or imagined dateman, where is he? In the mountains above the cloud line, he sits in small firelight hidden amid rock. This is what I think. He scratches his beard and waits. It is cold, but he has patience. He senses new energy. What does he want? How will he stir the pattern of things? But the village men say nothing will happen tonight. They say it under the covers to their wives. Nothing will happen. The land itself sometimes demands slumber. The most violent wars have unpredictable moments of peace, as if the world has said enough. Enough. Such pauses are few and brief, the trance passes and men and armies regather their hate and the columns move along the crooked roads and into the wheat. But you remember the quiet night. It is the only thing you can say is yours, even though you know it is only borrowed.

I cannot sleep. I can only imagine what I cannot see. My nights go by in hours like this. I am a restless scribe. When this began I don't know. Pills don't work, and booze is not the trick. It is only near dawn that my body finds its heaviness. I drift. You know that blissful drift, the one when you realize your next conscious thought will be in a room of morning light. You cross over, disappear from the world. When I was a boy, I tried to capture that moment. I forced myself to stay awake, hoping I could transport my waking mind into the sleep world. I could study it. I could live alongside the goblins and eroticism of a boy's dreams and touch that woman roaring by in her Cadillac and then stopping in front of me as a high heel clicked on the sidewalk and a long leg curved out the door. I walked toward her. I never saw her face. She hasn't come back in decades. I miss her. They say that when you die, the hidden faces in your dreams become known. They're your heaven or hell. I drift, and the night recedes. The gray light of dawn speckles the walls. Alija turns and curls away from me. I trace her spine with a finger. Our borders widen. The donkey cart is in spin again. The village men with their rifles have returned, tiny spoons clinking in their tea. The wives are happy. The fires lit. The wheat fields are dewy and slick. The night passed as promised. There's a bang on the door.

"Yo," says Brian. "Time for some breakfast."

We splash water and dress and soon are on the road.

"Let's go see Vijay," says Brian.

"I can't handle him this early."

"He knows shit, Jay."

"He's a boor, but I like him," says Alija.

"He talks —"

"Incessantly."

"Yes."

"He's got a few rebel contacts."

"And when has he ever provided them?"

"Jay, you gotta work the dude," says Brian.

Vijay's a good man; he's just a yakker. He edits a small weekly. The MUP shut him down every three or four days, and, when they're not doing that, they're kicking the shit out of Vijay's reporting staff. His English is British aristocracy washed through American street prose. Words flying and wisping, sharp-edged and rounded. Vijay wants a reprieve from this place and is hoping for a fellowship in the States, some "Ethics and the Press in War-Torn Countries" euphemism sponsored by journalist foundations looking to get academic with the world's nastiness. Why did my profession start taking itself so seriously? Fellowships are good to a point, but they spawn self-indulgence. I don't want to get too academic here, don't want to fall into the trap or become the canard myself, but hyperbole is killing the essence of simple, dogged reporting. Look at all those chattering people on all those talk shows all jousting one another and saying nothing. Nothing. Sunday morning in the States is a *Revenge of the Journalists* movie. They're everywhere doing everything but journalism. They speculate, they ponder, they prattle in polemics. A monkey with a thesaurus can do it. I've never seen these hacks and pundits in the places I am. I only see them in TV studios, hair stiff as frost, pulling on their baritones, waddling around in makeup, talking about the places I am as if they know what they're talking about. You have to laugh. It's so grand and absurd to listen to these poodles whine breathlessly on because they're too lazy to do any real reporting. What happened to the purity? Muddled and corrupted. I am not bitter, though. This is the way of things, an evolution, I suppose, disturbing in the disturbing kind of way that suggests the premonitions of banshees to come. Yet, I must admit, I've written Vijay letters of recommendation to a few East Coast institutions. He's a hustler, and he deserves a break from the bullets and the burnings. Let him walk among the ivy, eat cold danish and drink weak coffee, let him spill his horrors and his secrets and perhaps bed a few academics before his stipend runs out.

"Jay, Brian, Alija. How wonderful to see you again. What is going on? What is happening? Two American journalists such as yourselves in my office at the same time. Am I missing something, Jay? Where should I dispatch my staff? The tiny war is growing with new secrets every day."

He laughs and his eyebrows dance.

"Nothing's going on. We're here to chat. What's news?"

"Jay, please, a little foreplay, huh? My office is dreary today. Let's go next door for a drink."

He slaps my back — "Ahh, Jay, it's so good to see you again" — and we funnel out his door. "Jay, I've heard from the Kennedy School. There may be something for me in the spring. Do you know that fellowship? It's a good one. I have friends in Boston. The home of the Tea Party. Jay, Jay, Jay, so good to see you, and we're having our own little Boston Tea Party right here in these mountains. Historic things, Jay. Historic things."

I can see Brian mimicking Vijay from behind. Alija joins in. He rattles on. A touch overweight, with flecks of gray in his goatee, Vijay moves in gentle, almost separate, rhythms as if the grid of neurons connecting his limbs and mind is slightly off kilter. It's barely noticeable, but Vijay never seems to walk in sync, yet he yaks so much that it all somehow comes together and he glides forth like a gregarious sailboat in spotty winds. We cross the street to his favorite café, and Vijay heads for his table. It wobbles in a crack of sunlight beneath a speaker playing a hybrid of techno-pop and Turkish funeral dirge.

"Let's have espresso and brandy."

"How are you, Vijay?" says Brian.

"I'm well, considering. The MUP come too often and smash up my office."

"Why don't they shut you down?"

"Haven't you heard? This is a democracy. A free press is welcome. There's a sheen of respectability over this madness, Brian."

"Jesus, Vijay, you are ready for Harvard."

"How many dead in the last two weeks?"

"Nobody knows. But there's a lot of freshly turned earth out in the villages. Alija, any word from your brother?"

"Nothing."

"If he is in the mountains, he's safe for now. The rebels aren't good fighters yet, but they know the land."

"We watched them ambush a MUP checkpoint the other night."

"They want a war of body counts. If one or two MUP are killed every couple of days, that begins to add up, and maybe the MUP will get tired of fighting what they cannot see."

"Or burn down a lot more villages."

"The more likely outcome."

A reed-thin kid in an apron brings our drinks. Vijay swirls his brandy and sips his espresso. *One, two three, four . . .* I count the seconds. Vijay often departs from events at hand and reminisces over his first brandy. *Five.*

"I danced with a countess once," he says. "I was a child. Very small. Things were prosperous, and my father took us on vacation to the Croatian coast. A beautiful coast of

scattered islands. We were at a little restaurant eating calamari and looking at the sea. As a child, Jay, I loved calamari.
Isn't that odd? After I ate, I whirled around the floor to the
tune of this tiny band. I must have been very cute, because
suddenly a woman appeared and took me by the hands and
danced with me. She was beautiful. Her hair pulled back,
her skin brown, and gold on her wrist. She laughed and
hugged me when the music stopped and went away. My father later told me she was a countess from a country I no
longer remember. I had a picture, but I must have lost it."

"The closest I got to royalty was a homecoming
queen," says Brian.

"How about you, Jay?"

"I only ever danced with girls. Unadorned but lovely
girls."

"I never danced," says Alija. "Between religious customs
and the MUP, Friday nights aren't much fun."

"Jay will dance with you," says Vijay. "When all this is
over, Jay, you must promise to dance with Alija."

"I'm sure Alija would rather dance with someone
younger."

"You're not so bad," he chides. "But there is a bit more
gray in your hair. Am I right?"

"You have a cruel eye, Vijay."

"Yes, I do." He laughs.

"Vijay, what's happening out there? Don't be coy."

"Has talk of countesses and homecoming queens run
its course? Another brandy, huh?"

"Vijay."

"There are new personalities."

72

"Official? Unofficial?"

"I would say more freelance."

"Mercenaries?"

"In the mountains. A few retired Special Forces I'm told. They read those Georgia magazines you Americans have with stories about bullets, hardware, and trajectory. They're paid well."

"Training?"

"What else?"

"How many guerrillas?"

"Five, six thousand."

"That's not enough."

"Not to win a war, but to provoke a larger one."

"NATO," says Alija.

"Kaboom."

"The West can't have the Balkans go nuts again. Poor Europe would have a collective heart attack. Remember Sarajevo. No one was paying attention and death was piling up, and then a mortar lands in a marketplace and there's bodies all over. TV swooped in and people had to take notice. Suddenly Bosnia went prime time. It's like slowly adding weights. One day, the scales tip."

"They didn't tip in Rwanda."

"Leave Africa aside."

"Naturally."

"One day there'll be one village burned too many."

"You're stating the obvious," says Brian. "We know this. We've seen the Chevy Suburbans. The people at the U.S. mission here say they're just monitoring things. That's bullshit. They're more active. Have you seen these guys?"

"Not personally, no."

"How do you know, then?"

"My guerrilla friends. Don't be so naive, Brian. I grew up with many of the armed men in the mountains."

"Why aren't you with them?"

"We each have our special task. Jay has a friend in the mountains too, don't you, Jay? I keep waiting for that story. Jay knows a secret man. What does he say? So many new personalities in the mountains. Official. Unofficial."

I look into my espresso. Alija glances away. I wasn't going to talk about Rolo here. I wasn't going to talk about Rolo anywhere. Vijay is one of those wonderful creatures of war, those guys who navigate chaos and somehow survive and even prosper. He's a chimera, a man of grafted allegiances, spread out and playing a game, watching characters flit across his landscape. He could be your best friend and be sleeping with your enemy at the same time. I don't want to get too cynical or paranoid, a most annoying trait among hacks, but Vijay, as much as I enjoy his nostalgic asides about countesses and seashores, is as shifting and elusive as smoke. Indecipherable.

"I see we have come to a lull in the conversation," says Vijay.

"Hey, where can I fish around here?"

"The best rivers are west toward the mountains."

"What else is in the mountains?"

"I think you mean who, don't you, Jay?"

"You're so precise in your English."

"It's a crafty language. So many little alleys."

"So?"

"There is a guest from far away."

"You sound like a parable. This guy real or imagined?"

"Terribly real."

"Terribly?"

"The MUP aren't the biggest problem. The MUP are doing what they've always done. But their ideology is gone. They hate, but they've lost the poetry of why. The MUP are working designs of the past world. They don't fit into the new one, and there is a new world, Jay. This man has ideas. He wants war against a way of life, not against an army. He and others like him want your soul. These little mountains are a proxy diversion for him. He's looking for followers. I love the word *proxy*, the way it slices through the mouth. *Proxy*."

"Have you seen him?"

"Only a few have seen him."

"Where's he from?"

"There's much speculation. I really don't know."

"What about the dates?"

"I love that allusion. The bearded man and his dates."

"Is it true?"

"Always looking for that nice bit of color, huh, Jay? It doesn't matter if it's true. It's part of the new mystery. I was in some villages the other day. This man is all people are talking about."

"So," says Brian, "let me get this straight. There's some whack job out there with a beard and a bag full of dates who's decided to stir up a little mischief here? This is good. I like this. Much better than the MUP. I agree with you, Vijay, the MUP have become passé. Their massacres have the taint of redundancy."

"I like your facetiousness, Brian."

"Jay was holding back on me."

"I was going to tell you."

"Cancel my Fiji vacation. We have jihad in the mountains."

"It may not be religious. But guys with dates tend to speak immortality."

"Masquerade religion."

"Who makes such distinctions? People are inspired by generalities, not specifics."

"The Muslims here won't go for it. Holy war won't sell."

"This is a land ready for any kind of war, Jay."

"Vijay's right," says Alija. "Why not? Everything else has failed. You tell people they're part of the West, but you don't give them the rights of the West. You tell them to be patient and peaceful, but all they get is beaten. Why won't people look elsewhere?"

"Why haven't you written about him, Vijay?"

"He's too dangerous to write about now. Too much still unknown about him."

"Can we get to him?"

The waiter appears, and Vijay waves him off. Brandy shines in Vijay's glass. He leans back in his chair. Brian makes some notes and Alija combs her hair and then she and Vijay whisper things. The café is filled with young men and girls. They look at one another across sticky tables. Hands hold hands, hands rub cheeks, clicks of brief kisses, smiles and giggles. Cigarettes and espressos and Camparis. This is foreplay for Muslim girls whose fathers want them chaste. The techno-pop-Turkish-funeral-dirge music veers into Blondie, and the café taunts the young couples with forbidden sexuality. They are so pretty, and war is upon them. The fighting in the countryside will come to the city, and all the virgins will be scattered, and all their young men, these boys in black leather jackets and scuffed shoes, will have to choose the rifle or the grave or both. Let them linger. Why not? Vijay collects his papers and snaps back a cold espresso. He rises, and we follow his jangled gait out the door and up the sidewalk.

"I must work before the MUP come and trash me again," he says.

"We'll see you soon."

"Perhaps."

Chapter 8

Perhaps.

So much unknown. We drift out there with instincts and a faint map. What is true? What is not? Can you find it anyway? Write one true sentence. Somebody said that once. But does it exist? Can syllables and sounds make truth? Is language capable of such precision? I think not. The best we get is a composite. We don't even know the truth about ourselves. How do we find it beyond? Look at me. Bleeding bank accounts, laughable portfolios, apartments, fires, domestic messes, too much drink, too little rest, plane tickets, hotels, customs guards with crookedly sewn patches, lost computers, missed interviews, bulletproof vests, endless fights with editors, but in the end all I need is twelve to fifteen hundred words and I can compress the world for you. I can move characters like God. Admittedly, it's a tiny stage. A few columns of newsprint wedged between ads for underwear and jewelry. That grid of black type is my best stab at the truth. It is the place I am most honest. My confessional. It's not as hallowed as it sounds. Twining threads, making rope. Facts, details, color twisted together. Describe a face, the lift of a cup, a gesture of motivation. Documents. I love documents. They add gravity to the human element. Collecting, collecting. Twisting, twisting, twisting. The story comes. A languid lede, or one with the power of a sucker punch? Keep it moving. Character, color, creating place. Hit the nut hard. The nut graph is what it's all about. Why are you telling this story? What's it mean? What's the frequency, Kenneth? Then let it ride, but never use all your notes. If you use everything in the notebook, you're a shitty reporter. You have to leave half out. That's the deal. That means you got the details. You got it right. But is it true? That's the annoying rub. There is a man in the mountains. This we know. But why? For what purpose? Even if you meet this willowy, bearded character with dates, will you get the truth? *Willowy*? Where did *willowy* come from? He wasn't willowy before. Why now? See, layers added and you didn't know. That's the thing. A story widens. It gathers like a storm. Things appear invisibly. Who added *willowy*? Vijay? Alija? Brian? Me? Now *willowy* will be out there. It will become part of the lexicon of this man no one has seen. He may be short and fat, but for now he is somehow willowy. And he is bringing war. No, scratch that. He is the thread in a larger war. Maybe not a decisive thread, but still a thread. He needs to be twisted into the narrative. He needs to be defined. God must plunk him on the stage and introduce him to the world.

"Let's eat," says Brian.

"Mixed grill?"

"What else."

"Chewy brown stuff on a stick."

"We should be covering Wall Street, Jay."

"Nice clothes. Good lunches."

"Knicks tickets."

"Chinatown in the rain."

"Yes, Jay, we blew it. Got in the wrong line when they were picking teams."

"Cut it out," says Alija.

"Why? We were just imagining."

"I can't imagine. It's all make-believe to me."

"No context."

"Only videos. You have basketball games. I have sheep shit and dust."

"Poetic."

"She's been watching British films."

"La-di-dah," says Brian.

"Better dialogue," says Alija.

"You know what British movie I did like? *Chariots of Fire*. Remember those guys running on the beach in their white shorts?"

"I loved that," says Alija.

"You can get *Chariots of Fire* here?"

"We get all kinds of movies. Smuggled in from Macedonia. You can get anything, Brian," says Alija. "You can get a Russian whore if you want."

"They're too intimidating. I like Romanian whores. Black-market. Jay, that's —"

Boom. Mortar rounds are profound conversation stoppers. I swerve, and we slide into a ditch on the hillside outskirts of the city. Boom. Another lands in a field in a spray of dirt and stone. Smoke. Whoosh, boom. Another. The sound, so pure and pristine, permeates beyond tissue to bone, traveling up the spine in a knot and across the shoulders. Other cars skid into the ditch. We climb out of the Jeep. No one is hit, only a few shrapnel nicks in the back door. Broken watermelons scatter the road, and a donkey attached to its cart is lying with a torn leg. It wails and struggles to rise in spastic kicks. Blood trickles from its nose. The people are okay, but the donkey stepped onto a precise place at a wrong time and caught whirling metal. Its matted coat is singed; strands of white smoke rise from its body. It's so random it makes you believe in fate. The animal's owner ambles muddy from the ditch. He looks around: green rind, seeds, and red pulp at his feet. Someone hands him a gun. He looks down. Two pops. The donkey shudders, and there is a wire of air like when a window closes, and then the cart and the hooves and all motion ceases. Eleven men unharness the animal and drag it to the roadside. Children skip and laugh through the split melons. The cart is turned upright and trotted away by two boys. Cars are pulled from the ditch, mortar-round marks are studied, heads shake, and life, temporarily frozen in fear, subsides to its rhythms, and soon the jumble moves on, the kaleidoscope turns, and the scene is as it was moments before the first explosion, except for the paintbrush stroke of blood that will remain until the evening rain.

A few guys help us push our Jeep out of the ditch. We give them a little cash, and they walk whistling down the road and toward a city streaked by fog. Brian, Alija, and I say nothing. The Jeep smells of fresh dirt, a tinge of gunpowder. We don't know who fired the mortars. It could have been the MUP. It could have been the guerrillas attempting to blame the MUP for a few civilian casualties. Or it could have been some kids with an old tube and a few shells. We drive away.

Megan sits at the bar. It's been a while. Maybe five years ago in some Bosnian shit hole with a crunch of consonants for a name. She is a sight, lifting her beer in the chatter and smoke at the end of the day. There are more journalists and NGO types here than a few weeks ago. The scent is out. The waiters in their clip-on bow ties and snug black vests are happy. The gangsters and the money changers are jolly too. Alija is right. You can get it all. The anticipation of bloodshed does magical things. Opportunists of all denominations have suddenly appeared. Money belts will fatten and prices will rise. Translators — shrewd sensors of changing economic indicators — will bump themselves from one hundred to two hundred dollars a day. Gas spirals. Hotels get ridiculous. Cologne masks the scent of sheep, and everyone's a businessman in a bad suit with a leering eye. It's like Bogart in that bar in Casablanca, only not as suave or seamless. No one's ordering champagne, either. This is strictly beer and whiskey. Two Russian hacks are sitting in the corner, wearing cutoff shorts and getting drunk. Brian thinks he recognizes them from Chechnya and goes to say hello. An Italian I know from somewhere is sitting with a British spook I know from somewhere else. Whisper, whisper. Local pols are looking grave and sanguine in the corner. UN monitors sit neatly in their sweaters, downcast eyes and plastic smiles. And who is this? Ahhh, the let's-drive-down-the-dirt-road freelancer with the porcelain nose and the patrician grin. Ellen's still alive, I see. She's washed her T-shirt and traded bandana colors. Her sidekick, Ted, is hovering with a highball glass and a cigarette; the guy's too nervous, looks perpetually cold. He's eavesdropping on a couple of old hacks who made their careers in other wars and are now writing books that will glimmer for a moment and then tumble forever into the bargain box. I read their stuff years ago, and they were good, awfully good, but you can never be too good for too long, and by the time the cult of recognition rises the best you'll ever do is gone. The door keeps opening, and people keep arriving. The stew is thickening. The bartender is running out of glasses and sweating. Another case of something is delivered. The beer tap hisses, and foam splatters the worn marble counter, and everyone seems hallucinatory in a grimy mirror. A clutch of thugs — all wearing the same black shoes with off-center gold buckles — are doing shots of raki and hugging one another, red-faced and weeping at being out with friends with a good seat by the window, watching the traffic and thinking they own a part of something. Then one of them will say something about someone's sister, and the brotherhood will dissolve into badly thrown punches before a gun is pulled and some semitoothless cousin gets shot in the knee or the abdomen. I can see the future with this crowd, my dysfunctional family on the road to war.

"Buy me a drink?"

"You buy me a drink."

"We're both on expense accounts."

"How romantic."

"How are you?"

"Same as before."

"You look great."

"Jay, if I don't look great in this crowd it's time to join a nunnery."

"Can you still do that? I thought all the nunneries closed."

"I saw your byline and figured I'd run into you."

"How's Doctors Without Borders?"

"Ready to heal," says Megan.

"I heard you were in Africa."

"Rwanda for a while. I took a long time off after that. Had a friend with a house on the Maldives."

"I could use that about now," I say.

"It's coming, huh?"

"I think. Where are you setting up?"

"Still mapping it out," says Megan. "Probably somewhere toward the mountains."

"Look around. How many faces do you know?"

"A few."

"We travel in a small world," I say.

"Is that Brian over there with those Russians?"

"Yeah."

"He looks thinner."

"Runs on nerves."

"He suffers from sat-phone anxiety, as I recall."

Megan laughs. The daughter of a man with a lot of silos, she is from the Midwest and a graduate of NYU medical school. She worked in a city hospital for a year and then joined DWB and has been trundling through war and famine ever since. There's a tribe of people like her, disap-

84

pearing into the raw world, leaving former identities in a box or a basement and sending short notes home every now and then to families who tell neighbors that their daughter is altruistic, if a bit odd. I don't remember where it was that I first slept with Megan. She was a kind soul even in bed, and when she came she would weep and almost melt through my skin. She approached everyone with an aura of sympathy, as if we all — from a hacked-up African to a horny journalist — had lost our way and needed a hand to guide us back to the intended road. I'll bet as a child she wandered the Midwest dusks looking for Daddy's lost cattle. This is not to suggest she isn't selfish, because she is. Everyone here is selfish, and Megan is selfish in her goodness. The complexities of that are too tedious to ponder at the moment. I just want a few whiskies and quiet patter with my old but new again girlfriend. I want to give a waiter a big tip so he'll remember me and I'll be set until the war is over. I feel rich. I have somebody else's money in my pockets. I have a new computer and a fully charged sat-phone battery. The green light is on. The connection to the big world is static free. I can send words and words and words; I am a limitless dispenser of information. But I don't want to file tonight. I want to sleep with a girl I can enter. Alija is fine, and I can hold her and feel her and in some ways I am more intimate with her than with anyone before, but I need to be inside and she won't give me that, not yet, and I understand why, but still, I have needs, I am selfish for things. A beer bottle drops. A pop and a pause, and then the bar swirls on, and the mortars and the dead donkey fade, and the rain comes as promised and the blood is washed away in the night and Brian is drunk as he and the Russians build a toothpick castle on their table in the corner.

Morning. Light beautiful and cruel. Megan sleeps in a room I suppose is in a hotel. I don't remember much of last night. Megan's suitcase — bursting with clothes like a stuffed doll ripped — sits on a chair. She rolls over and finds me. I am on my back looking at the cracks in the ceiling, pretending it's a big map, looking for a brittle edge to take me someplace. Someplace new. I think of the wall of maps in the Vatican. Painted in gold and blues, the sketches depict the evolving world as man understood it through the centuries. In each succeeding map, the lines are more precise, the contours of the coastlines more accurate, the mountains rising, the blush of deserts, the world coming into focus in a slow, almost sensual way. Megan is warm. That is what I love most — the naked morning warmth of another, the breath and half-smile of a new day, the let's-get-coffee chatter, the splashing in the bathroom, when the makeup and the gloss of the night before are peeled away and we see things as they are, and, if we are lucky, those things will be the best.

Alija disappeared last night with friends to search for her brother and spend time on the town before we go to the mountains. I'll have to extricate Brian from the Russians. They could be anywhere. Megan sits up and walks toward the window, her body a silhouette in the sherbet orange curtain light. I have a theory. All terrible hues in the world end up in places like this, as if color-blind decorators with macabre tendencies were set loose in a contest to see who could be the most creative with the shards and nubs at the bottom of a crayon box. Megan is pretty even in this. Bodies. Alija's is tight, an iris on a stem. The corners of her eyes, her breasts, her hips are as a young God intended when he pulled a rib from Adam and shaped clay in the garden. In Alija's body I see my own age, the lines and curves I once was, the diminishment of what I have become. Alija is a girl of instinct, and when she lies with me on those nights of her choosing she is light upon me and quickly sets herself to the rhythm of my breathing. She seems able to disperse and then regather along my side, her warmth creeping over me, her head high on my chest, strands of her hair catching the stubble of my chin. Some men want to possess such a body, but you cannot. It's a prayer of pleasure you will never own. Megan's body tempts in different ways. It is an achievement of wisdom. Her skin is softer, pliable, the slight puff of belly, the aureole a whorl of tenderness. I prefer Megan's body. Its wants are more, its desires harder to please, but it is understanding and forgiving, and like mine, its muscle and tone are deeper, its imperfections are the very things that make it alluring. It is a body that has survived youth and has found things on the curious road toward mortality.

"I'm hungry."

"Eggs and cheese and half-ripe tomatoes."

"Why are tomatoes never fully ripe here?"

"I don't know, but I know a place that serves a decent espresso."

"It's all in the machine."

"The grind."

"No, Jay, the machine. It's all about steam and compression. Ask any Italian."

The science and mathematics of espresso making are, I suppose, interesting, but not today. Megan leaves the window and lies beside me. We make love in the tacky light. When she comes her body shudders like a light breeze riffling an awning. She's on top and she holds my face in her hands, squeezing slightly, kissing. She pushes back my hair. She doesn't cry. She seems happy, and I think that maybe she has retreated, maybe she has realized that only a little of the world can be healed. We leave the room and head for food. Brian sits with three espresso cups in front of him.

"Goddamn Russians."

"Why do you even try to hang with them?"

"Pride, Jay. C'mon, we grew up in the Cold War. Remember the Olympics? We duked it out with the Russians medal for medal."

"Gymnastics is one thing, but vodka and Russians — you're a dead man. You're wiped."

"They did me in. The worst part, Jay, they got up hours ago laughing like two kids. Goddamn Russians. They only have one computer between them, so they were fighting all night about who gets to use it today."

"You remember me?"

"Yes, I do, Megan. How are you?"

"I'm well."

"Africa?"

"Rwanda."

"That's as ugly as the human soul gets."

"So far."

"Let's eat."

We sit. Eggs on silver plates, a strange jelly and bread toasted on one side.

"Hey, look, in the corner, it's Tobias Brookstone III."

"Not him."

"In the flesh."

"Who's Tobias Brookstone?"

"A fiction writer pretending to be a journalist."

"He makes stuff up?" says Megan.

"Let's call it healthy embellishment. Once, I forget where, he wrote this overheated lede that said war was 'only days if not hours away.' There was a problem. The war came six months later."

"Tobias is going to be looking for the dateman, Jay."

"He'll interview him even if he doesn't find him."

"It'll read like this: 'U.S. and Western intelligence officials are concerned that a new, troubling dynamic has injected itself into the civil war in . . . yada, yada, yada.'"

"Tobias does order the best wine, though."

"This is true."

"He always picks up the tab."

"True again."

"He's kind of, in a slightly perverse way, charming."

"Affected."

"You mean the accent?"

"The William Buckley School of Affected Speech."

"Good espresso," says Megan.

"Told you."

"Hey, Brian, what makes a good espresso?"

"The machine, man. Everyone knows that."

Chapter 9

We are in the wheat on a cloudy' night.

"Jesus, Jay. What are we doing?"

"Getting muddy. Shhhhhhhh."

The Serbs didn't want to invite us, but here we are, the guests of Milan the sniper. The guerrillas have grown bold. They burn Serb fields in the night. Milan and thirty other men gather in the dusk at the village barn. They draw in the dirt, assigning patrol routes and handing out guns and flashlights. A few get grenades. One crazy bastard has a scythe. Then they disappear, slipping shadows through the furrows. This land and its divided people know how to be quiet. The guerrillas roll across the countryside in silent waves, and the Serbs, a boisterous lot in a bar, are as swift and mute as water bugs when protecting their land. Whispers coil through the wheat, hand signals flash, and when darkness comes footsteps turn to soft, slow patter. Brian, however, is about as stealthy as a garbage truck.

"This is like duck season in Michigan."

"That's not your line. I've heard it before."

"I stole it from a guy at *The News*."

"I know that guy. He's got this calmness about him. He files great stuff and never misses lunch."

"I always miss lunch. I can't see, Jay. I think it's going to rain."

"Shhhhhhh. Take some notes."

Megan and I said good-bye hours ago. She's on her way to a small clinic in the mountains. Alija is back in the city buying jeans for herself and gumdrops for village kids. I think she sometimes slips them money, too. She doesn't think I notice but she never gives me the change from the stuff we buy. I'd like to have her here tonight, but no small platoon of angry Serb farmers is going to trust an Albanian translator. We have hired Marko. He has a pallid face and spiky dyed blond hair; he looks like a ghost Serb. He's from Belgrade. The farmers don't trust him and they speak to him in terse snippets, partly because they're jittery in the dark wheat and partly because Marko reminds them of a misbehaving dog. The quotes could be a lot better, but not all days are victories, and, besides, the scene is what makes this story. Brian knows this, too. A lot of hacks don't understand reinvention. They get set on how they think a story should be. But things change, lands shift, and the day planned in the morning often veers another way. Stories are everywhere, and the best often hide in the unexpected. Do I sound like a sage? I am not. I just know where luck comes from.

Rain rattles the fields. Brian was right. I tuck my notebook into my jacket, Marko's spikes are wet and wilted, and although he'd rather be interviewing girls at a dance club, he's intrigued among these gruff, rustic men. Eight hundred acres. That's what the farmers will patrol tonight. Their great-grandfathers guarded the land before them. Blood and seed, blood and seed, through the generations. I feel for them, though. Victims of geography and nationalist politics, they are outnumbered nine to one by the Albanians. All they want is to farm, to break soil and grind wheat in Milan's water mill and to end each day with a stinging sip of plum brandy. But their government's "policy" on Albanians brought an uprising that will likely chase them from their land. This may be the Serb farmers' final harvest. Some will die fighting; others will load the coffins of their ancestors onto hoods of cars and flee in a broken, weepy circus, meandering down the highway with the maps and bones of history. The new owners will burn the fields, scrape away the purified ash, and plant different crops. This is what I'm composing in my head. It's a bit premature, a little too much analysis; the final harvest may be a touch dramatic. I'll have to tone it back when I write, but in the end this is what will happen.

"Jay, you're wet."

"You're pretty soggy yourself, Milan."

"I am a man of the elements."

"Anything moving?"

"No, it's quiet. The rain helps."

Milan's rifle is slick and shiny. It seems a part of him.

"My uncle used to say that wind through the wheat made the fields look like the sea."

"I could imagine that."

"Sometimes, Jay, I get tired of this shit."

"You have a lot of enemies."

"We made some, inherited others."

He hands me the rifle.

"Lift it and look through the scope."

"It's dark. I won't see anything."

"Just lift it."

The scope was like a miniature dripping tunnel.

"What do you see?"

"A telephone pole. It's blurry."

"But your vision is narrow, right?"

"Yeah, just tight on the pole."

"That's what I like about it, Jay."

"What do you mean?"

"History brought us here. I know the future will look different, and soon new things will come and years will pass and things will be repeated. All I have is now. Get it? What's in the scope. The narrow vision of the scope is all I care about. I follow it. It protects me. Protects my family."

I lower the rifle and hand it back. We slip under a tree. Milan cups his hand and lights a cigarette. He is unshaven and pale, a small armory of a man with a knife in his boot, a bandolier over his shoulder, a pistol in his back pocket, and his rifle leaning at his side. We listen. I hear the clop of a donkey cart on the distant road. Two farmers walk up to us. They don't speak. Milan hands them a water bottle, and they recede back to the rim of wheat. Another man arrives minutes later and leans toward Milan's ear. Milan grabs his rifle. We run for about three hundred meters on the dirt road. Milan and I follow the man into the wheat. I feel swallowed. The mud is thick, and I hear voices. I look for pricks of light in the dark, but there are few. We are out of the wheat, running on another dirt road. Other farmers are running too. Some lumber, others are swift. They are one with the darkness and everything is hard to see, blurs and brief moments of precision and blurs again. The guy with the scythe trips in a curse and a splash in the furrows. Farmers are jostling beside me. Guns are drawn but no one is firing. Quick breaths, quick breaths. Milan runs into a small clearing and stops near a tractor. Rain and sweat. The other men arrive and Kalashnikovs are raised. Someone laughs, and I hear a squish.

"Goddammit, Ratko."

"Bastard."

"Idiot."

A flashlight clicks on. This man named Ratko sits in the mud with a bottle, drunk and squinting. The other men surround him. Two guys lift him up and guide him away.

"Carry on, men," says Ratko, turning his head back toward us. "If you see a guerrilla, by all means shoot."

Another laugh. Rifles are lowered. Ratko, I am told, is the village caretaker. He tends the church graveyard and is an expert roofer. A refugee from the earlier Bosnian war, he arrived in the village one day with no money and a bag of tools. He hid his drinking habit for a while, but with a new war coming he is less inclined to secrecy and is often fished out of the wheat. The farmers are pissed but grateful for Ratko's diversion: a spasm of excitement but no death. They disperse again into the darkness. Brian and Marko wander away with a couple of them. Milan and I head back to the tree. There's a crack in the clouds, and moonlight makes brief silhouettes of the church and the water mill. The moon quickly vanishes and it's black again and the men are scattered across the acres and the wheat is heavy with rain and the rain keeps falling and the ink in my notebook runs and disappears and it's as if I've never been here at all. Milan and I spread out some plastic and sit. He hands me a flask. The taste is sweeter than usual, and Milan tells me he's experimenting with sugar, heat, and fermentation. He laughs that he'll become a rich man, a jazz-playing exporter of brandy. Maybe so. War takes men far away from themselves, and maybe Milan does have a jazzman's or a tycoon's soul. Who knows? I cannot see him as anything but a sniper, but this is unfair even though that is how he came to me years ago in the mountains outside Sarajevo. He stands and scans the wheat. He doesn't want to see a rustle. He doesn't want a battle in this messy weather. He comes back and sits next to me against the tree. The rain keeps falling, and Milan talks until I don't hear him anymore. Dawn is a foggy affair. My ass is soaked. Milan is up, smoking in the haze along the edge of the field. The wheat is safe for another day.

A bearded man in robes with a cross dangling from his chest whisks past, and Milan motions for me to follow. The other farmers are on the road too. I see Brian and Marko. We gather at the church. The holy man slides a key in the door. We step in, wet and muddy beneath mosaics of Saint George slaying the dragon and John the Baptist along the shoals of the Jordan. Bits of mosaic are missing, mildew seeps across the ceiling. Broken stained glass has been replaced by colored cellophane. The altar cloth is frayed and yellowed. The priest lights a candle, and incense wisps amid our foul clothes. He raises his arms and says the night has been good, the men have been brave, and the enemy, fearing God and the righteous, has been kept away. But the village must not weaken in this vigil, he says. Another night is coming and another night after that. There is no time to be tired. God lifts the spirits of the courageous. The wheat is growing strong, but it is fragile amid the acts of men. God made it so. God made battlefields, and God made children, and one is needed to protect the other. The priest doesn't conjure parables from the Bible. He speaks in the present as if new plagues and new wars are being writ that will centuries from now be re-membered. He is wise. He needs to do this. Man wants to live in an epic. How else would he have the balls to arm himself and walk into the night? The priest raises his gold cross. The saints arch overhead, and we seem a strange com-munion of souls in this teapot of a church. The men bow their heads for a final blessing. The priest lowers his arms and makes a joke about Ratko. Everybody laughs. Milan and the farmers go home to sleep, except for the man with the scythe, who sweeps mud and water from the church as the fog lifts and the wheat shimmers, like an imagined sea, in the breeze.

Chapter 10

"Took you long enough."

"Rolo, you get harder to find."

"A man on the move, Jay. Hi, Alija."

"Hi, Rolo."

"Want to dance?"

"Maybe later."

Rolo's camped in a barn on a ridge. His guides keep watch. His computers and global positioning system bleep on a table. Rolo's happy and spins around like a little knot of energy. He hands Alija and me some tea and passes a bowl of olives. He unfolds a map and spreads it out on the dirt floor. He kneels his compact body down, and I am going to glimpse a speck of American intelligence. Just a speck. Rolo's not some Philly girl on a dark couch; he's not going to give me all his charms in one night.

"Your man with the beard and the dates is here."

"We knew that."

"Yeah, but you haven't seen him. He's fog and air. There and gone."

"You saw him?"

"Don't need to see him now. Somebody else saw him for me."

Rolo pulls a picture out of his vest and hands it to me. Slightly to left of center, between two guerrillas cleaning their rifles in what looks to be lantern light, there he is, the dateman, his beard hanging gauzelike over his collarbone, a scarf around his head, his nose slender, almost regal, and eyes downcast, reading a book. He wears an old green Army coat that seems too large for his frame, and the yellow lantern light brightens him in a beam of clarity that doesn't extend to the shadowed, almost out-of-focus men around him.

"How'd you get this?"

"Jay, please, you embarrass me."

"You have somebody in there, don't you?"

"Alija, more sugar?"

"No thanks, Rolo."

"Where was it taken?"

"Okay, Jay. You can't use any of this yet. No shit. I'm not kidding around. I'll let you know when you can use it. But now, just sit on it."

"Rolo, as you may have noticed, there's a lot of journalists rooting around these days."

"No one's going to get to this guy. He's way deep in the mountains."

"What's the deal?"

"He came from Afghanistan. We don't exactly know when. He's the son of some Arab sheik. He's spent time in the Sudan, and he may have had something to do with the U.S. embassy bombing in Tanzania. He's a moth. We can't get a fix on him. He floats in and out of places, but this is the first time he's been tracked to Europe."

"Was he invited?"

"We don't know. I would guess not. He brought a lot of money, though. And, yes, he did bring two donkeys loaded with dates. That's his shtick. He likes the whole Allah aura thing. He's clever. He knows these guerrillas don't have it pulled together yet. Poorly trained, underfunded. And then he arrives, sort of a mystic, a soft-spoken warrior, well, more a tactician, with money, maps, and ideas of something big."

I point to the picture.

"Is that the Koran he's reading?"

Rolo laughs.

"No. You know what this is? It's the goddamn U.S. Special Forces booby-trap and guerrilla war manual printed in 1969 in Carlisle, Pennsylvania. The bastard stole our stuff."

"If you have someone inside who can get a photo of him, why don't you take him out?"

"We want to watch this guy. He's intriguing. I mean, he's reading our playbook. He's getting into our head."

"You sound smitten."

"It's a challenge. Remember when Achilles fights Hector at Troy."

"You know, when you say Achilles with that Boston accent, it's a weird sound. It's like the double l is getting hung up between your teeth and tongue."

"Well, screw you. That's pretty clear, huh? Alija, why do you hang out with this twerp?"

"He says he's rich."

"He's a hack, he's not rich."

"Are you rich, Rolo?"

"Alija, I have money buried all over. I'd dig it all up for you."

Rolo pours more tea.

"I don't get why this guy is resonating here. These people aren't religious. They're not zealots. They're farmers and barbers and shop owners and an occasional heroin smuggler. They sip beer on the mosque steps."

"True enough. We don't know how much he'll impact. Maybe it's only temporary. Maybe they reject him tomorrow, the next day. Who knows? But somebody's listening to him. That's why we'd rather watch him than take him out."

"An insect on your pin."

"World Trade Center. 1993. Big bombs, well planned. Tanzania. 1998. Very nicely planned. These guys are threading the world with wicked shit. They don't like us, and it has nothing to do with economic development and the disadvantaged—Middle East youth-frustration bullshit Washington keeps peddling. It's deeper, man. It's not like the Cold War and the Soviet Union. Nobody wanted to press the red buttons. But these guys, Jay, these guys are all about red buttons."

"A spook who's spooked."

"I'm not kidding. These guys are different. Patient and conniving as all hell."

Rolo folds his map and rises from the dirt floor.

"Want to eat goat?"

"No, we'd better go. Where you headed next?"

"Time to go deeper into the mountains. You should start heading that way too. Alija, you have a sleeping bag?"

"A couple in the Jeep."

"There's a changed world coming, Jay. It's taking form in little shit holes like this around the planet. It's a new math."

"Right now all that new math is capable of doing is burning Serb wheat fields and misdirecting mortars. The MUP can crush them whenever."

Alija snaps me a hard look. She doesn't like my analysis of the rebels, but she stays quiet.

"You're counting trees," says Rolo. "Look big picture, my friend."

"I do love your abstract CIA analogies."

"When I'm done sloshing around the woods and the jungles of this fine earth, I am going to write books. Intrigue novels. Cloak-and-dagger shit. I've got so many ideas. I'll move back to Boston, get a little place along the Charles. I could even crew."

"Rolo, you're a bus driver's son, man. You're not a sculler."

"Not at first glance."

Rolo builds a fire. Alija and I crisscross down the ridge toward the Jeep. The sky is autumn dusk, bright orange-yellow, retreating purple, streaks of sun against a gray template. Each color fused but separate, complementing the other. The land is hard. Ditches are cobwebbed in frost, and there's a chill in my feet. War will come in winter. Chapped hands and mortar shells, blood in the snow, a land too hard for digging, the last breath, visible, hanging above death like a puff of dandelion. Descending below the cloud line, the terrain unfolds in the varying browns of a female peacock, with flecks of yellow, magenta, and fire rust. This is the muted time. The time of hard starry nights, when nature is through with coddling. A bullet moves cleaner in winter, more precise. Milan told me this, and I believe him.

Alija's brother has not been found. Ardian is one of the missing. She asked about him at his university. No one knows. The rumor is he disappeared with a knapsack to join the fighters in the mountains. Where is that young man I have never met? Mass graves are lined with what we need to know but what we cannot fathom. The only solace is that a body is not alone. It is tangled, threaded, meshed with others, a limbo of unfortunates lingering a shovel scrape below the earth. Mass graves are seldom neat; the land doesn't accept them. But perhaps they are better than a lone body in a forest, a body with stiff upright arms, frozen in reaching for what was never attained. The face the color of flour, eyes open, mouth aslant. That dumbfounded look of a bullet to the chest. So many ways to end: slit, burned, vanished. Alija plays the scenarios one by one. She works with me to find her brother. She gives me words from the mouths of others, and I am the gas and wheels of her journey. It's a fair trade.

"Jay, it's okay that I gave Rolo the picture of my brother, right?"

"I suppose."

"Rolo might see him in the mountains."

"He might."

"He's just a kid."

• • •

The Jeep is cold. It cranks and whines before it starts. There is no snow in the air, but there should be; it is that kind of night. We head back to the city to retrieve Brian and pack supplies. The dateman. He is willowy. Some things are as we imagine. I am happy to know he is thin and bending. I am happy he is not myth. There is perspective now. The image will stay with me: a man in a too-big coat with a beard, black eyes, and a war manual. My story. I know the photograph Rolo showed me will be out someday. It will appear on CNN or the BBC. The TV camera will zoom in ever so slowly to the figure in the lantern light. A new demon will be born. He'll be described as inscrutable, "a mystery to intelligence officials," a man "waging a new kind of war," a man "fighting what officials tell us is a holy war," a man of "jihad born into a wealthy family whose fanaticism led him to the caves of Afghanistan and the deserts of Africa." And from sparse facts folklore will grow, and what I'm sure of now I won't be sure of then. The story will change. Hacks and pundits will become overnight experts. Everyone will presume to know the dateman. The photo will keep appearing. Islamists will emblazon it on T-shirts, *Frontline* will make it black and white and grainy, Larry King will opine ridiculously over it, and it will all get very breathless for a moment, but then, unless the dateman has new tricks, unless he gets warm and fuzzy with Oprah, he will get lost in the news cycle, a bit of packaged information competing for light against the newest liposuction horror story or the drama of a missing wife and a suspicious husband. He'll be discarded like Monica Lewinsky, a minor titillation in what Rolo would call a larger tragedy. That's why I have to get to the dateman soon. Windows are closing. In stories like this, there is only one interview with the subject in question. Don't ask me why. That's just how it works. That interview belongs to posterity. It is not all knowing and doesn't pretend to be. It is a brief, true glimpse, a bit of grist for the history books. It is important because the story will be co-opted by other forces, and what is fact will blur with what is not. The dateman will slip away like a flash of mercury. I am not bitter, but we live in a media pantomime of mistaken assumptions and calculated illusions; reality is fiddled and fingered until it becomes cartoon. It is a world where a picture of a mass grave is more important than the why of a mass grave.

"Sleep with me."

And so we do. Alija stretches her body against mine, beneath cool covers and darkness.

"Jay, let me tell you the story."

"The same one?"

"Yes, the same one," she whispers.

"Will you end it tonight?"

"No."

I close my eyes, and she begins; her breath smells of gumdrops.

"Remember, Jay, how I told you it began? They came that morning after the artillery. I still hear their boots on the dirt. I ran to the tree with my mother. We buried the money and silver, and, like I told you, we waited and we just kept hearing the scrape of boots and then we saw fire on the rooftops, and we knew, Jay, we knew . . ."

Chapter 11

Bang, bang, bang.

Who else?

"Morning, Brian."

"Let's boogie, Jay. Get your ass out of bed. Trip time. Morning, Alija."

"You're a strange man."

"Look, I got *Chariots of Fire.* Went out with the Russians to the black market again last night. We shopped. I'm packed. Let's go."

"You missed a spot shaving."

"Where?"

"Left side. Below the ear."

"I'm going to the mountains, Jay. I don't think it matters."

"Just making you aware."

The Jeep is gassed. We are moving. Brian insists on a last stop for bananas, crackers, water, and candy bars. The fog lifts and the city hardens, a sullen smudge of communist-socialist architecture whose defining features are thousands of windows with honeycombed steel inlays and podlike buildings resembling alien spaceships. This odd aesthetic is streaked by steam curling off a power plant and, farther out, the spackled mist and yellowish sulfur smoke hanging over the coal and iron mines. If you wrung the air out, you could make a small but impressive mountain with all the grit and chemical compositions that fluttered to the ground. Months ago, after a day spent walking hospital corridors with a doctor, a bird dog of a man with quick hands and indecipherable charts, I proposed a story on the region's miasma of cancer, emphysema, infant mortality, and cleft palate. My editors didn't want it. "It's off point," one of them said. "The story is the war." "Not if you have cancer," I said. "Jay, stick to the fighting. We don't want to take the reader in too many directions." I love the way he said *we*. This particular editor has never been overseas. I find it troubling that an assistant foreign editor has never been to Rome or Berlin, much less to Doha or Dubai. He bubbled up from the copydesk, which, depending on its veracity and temperament, can be a scary place or a well-designed bit of human machinery that can save you from making a fool of yourself. Peopled by the dictionary readers among us, the copydesk floats on the rim of news like a grammatical shark. It swims through stories, adding a comma here, putting a colon there, pondering the precise meaning of words such as *slightly insane*. What exactly does one mean by *slightly insane*? Isn't insane a full-blown condition? Can insanity be slight? Can we be sued for putting *slightly insane* next to someone's name? These are the conundrums of the copy-editor community. Thick books are consulted. Fellow copy editors are called upon to parse and ponder.

"Brian. One-word answer. Copy editors?"

I glance at him in the rearview as we race beyond the city's outskirts.

"Jay, why spoil this beautiful morning drive into the mountains? If I'm not talking directly to an editor, I'm not thinking about an editor. This philosophy works for me. But since you've mentioned copy editors, I dated one once. I wrote her a love poem. She corrected it. It made me queasy. You know what'd be a great porno movie plot: copy editor as dominatrix. She could spank reporters with rolled up atlases and make them utter past-perfect verb forms. She could whip them into licking the cover of *Elements of Style* and make them scream out things like, 'No pun intended!'"

"Her name would be?"

"The Comma Bitch."

"Nominative Nanny."

"Present Tense Tina and the —"

"You guys are sick."

A crowd gathers at the edge of a dirt road beneath a spiral of smoke. We stop. About twenty-five yards down the road a car is twisted and ripped in two, the metal beneath its paint exposed and shiny. A seat has been blown into a ditch. The steering wheel lies near a shallow gray-black crater, and dashboard wires hang in limp strands. Papers blow in the dirt and spin through thistle on the roadside; scents of gunpowder and sheep shit linger. A farmer tells Alija two Americans were in the car. He says he warned them not to go down the road. He is quite sure he cautioned them enough. He says someone mined it last night. Before he says more, I see her silhouette slumped on the driver's side. Head down, her blond hair blushed with blood, her nose perfect, Ellen, the well-bred Philadelphia freelancer, is dead. Ted, like the car, lies in halves, his torso on one side of the road, his legs on the other. I could imagine him protesting when she swung a hard right and called him a pussy. A flash and a boom. Death immediate. Land mines lurk half-hidden in dirt. They are laid in grids, and there is never only one. No one runs to Ellen and Ted. I call the U.S. mission on the sat phone and give names and details. They say they'll send someone. More farmers gather. Children peer from the grass and whisper their own curious assessments about bodies and bones and black spirits flying through the mountains. Alija gives them gumdrops. We wait. Clouds roll in, break, and roll away, and sunlight falls in unpredictable slants, on the car, the crater, the steering wheel, through the windshield and across Ellen's face, and, at least once, on Ted's ripped pants and burned legs.

A quiet ambulance arrives. Three locals get out — one with a minesweeper and two others with zipper bags. The minesweeper slips on headphones and leads the way, swirling his wand disk in front of him. The sweeper detects another mine about fifteen yards in. He marks it with a black flag; a murmur curls through the crowd. He sweeps around the car halves. Nothing. The two other men make notes. One of them snaps pictures, and when he is done he approaches Ellen, brushing back her hair, his translucent rubber gloves speckled with blood. He has never touched, nor will he again touch, a woman from Philadelphia. Not one like this one, anyway, a foolish girl with a sharp nose and notebooks full of scrawl. Her fair skin intrigues him. It is the fantasy of men here. Ellen's whiteness is mixed with the childhood freckles that fade into her skin like distant stars. She is a map, a constellation chart, and I'm sure that's why the man strokes her hair, to touch, even with rubber gloves, a patina so foreign and unattainable. I don't blame him. I thought I might have touched Ellen one day too. I thought that from the first time I met her with Ted on another dirt road. I didn't particularly like her. But where would we be if we touched only those we liked? We create imagined destinies for people, we hold a day or two, a gap here and there, for them to imprint something new upon our lives. They are brief; they are not the ones who remain. I had left a gap for Ellen, perhaps a night over whiskies after we had filed. Maybe we would have slept together. I don't know. She was young and in a rush to accumulate, to be the first with some shred of news, but what did it matter without context? She lacked resonance, and this is what makes it such a waste. A few days from now in a Greater Philly graveyard, Ellen will be buried and praised as a courageous journalist who sought truth and some sense of justice, some notion of dignity and human rights in what a silver-haired banker uncle will call a harrowing war zone. Bullshit. She was an opportunist. She probably — and I don't mean to be cruel — never wrote a compassionate paragraph unless it was calculated to enhance herself. Ego is no use here. It blocks necessary voices. The two men pull Ellen from the car. She's intact, all her trauma disguised, except the blood around her face and hair. She is lovely, I have to say *lovely*, draped in foreign arms like a slumbering schoolgirl. They lay her on the ground and unfold a

109

crinkly zipper bag. They lift Ellen; her legs slide in, then her arms, shoulders, and head. The zipper tugs, and the last of her I see is a flash of her nose. The men collect Ted quickly, scooping him up with a cinder shovel. An American in an SUV arrives. A nervous, aftershave-drenched State Department guy who I can tell is at the point in his career when he's beginning to realize that you must trudge through shit like this before they give you London or Paris.

"Did you know them?"

"We met not long ago. They were freelancers."

"Any contactables?"

"No."

"Don't worry, we'll get that. Shame, huh? Thanks for calling."

He snaps a few pictures and drives off. Dead bodies need files to accompany them on their journeys home. Ellen and Ted will be duly processed. A manila folder with an E PLURIBUS UNUM seal for each. If I die like them, I hope the natives, no matter where I am, burn my body and end it there. I don't want to be bagged and processed.

Alija, Brian, and I climb into the Jeep.

"Not the best omen," says Brian.

"Should we call someone in the States?" Alija looks to me.

"I wouldn't know who."

"What papers did she string for?"

"Pittsburgh and I think some small thing in New Hampshire."

"I don't want to just send their bodies out there," says Alija. "We should call, Jay."

"The guy from the mission has their passports. He'll track down their families. I'll phone my desk in a few hours and give them their names and ask them to make some calls."

We are quiet. News of Ellen and Ted will spread quickly. Hacks will take it as a lesson. Don't go down dirt roads. It won't deter, though. The rumblings in the fields and mountains will become more alluring. Death makes copy richer, paragraphs form more easily, and everything seems to quicken in an air of half-invented immediacy. We approach the final MUP checkpoint before the land wrinkles up into hills. Alija sits rigid with eyes straight ahead. Her MUP mask is on. Brian types notes into his laptop. I roll the window down and hand a MUP our identity cards and papers. He stares across me to Alija. He asks to see the registration for the Jeep. I hand it to him, and he disappears into a cinderblock shed. It's gray out and the MUP are cold, milling around an APC and a strip of barbed wire. A young MUP blows the embers of a smoldering stick fire in the mud. Three young men are handcuffed and sitting on the roadside. Kalashnikovs and bullets are at their feet. They are poorly dressed in ripped sweaters and jeans and camouflage jackets. Captured guerrillas in sneakers and buckle loafers. One is bleeding from the nose; another's eyes are puffy and nearly closed in yellow-blue tenderness. The MUP appears at my window.

"Ahh, I see you've noticed our new friends," he says in English.

"Guerrillas?"

"Bad men. Shits, really. They sneak around and try to

kill us. We have to catch them. We collect them like insects. Some are hard to catch. They are like that bug in the summer that lights up. What's the word in English?"

"Fireflies, lightning bugs."

"Yes, they are firefly shits."

"Where do you take them?"

"We have a place. But it is dangerous out here. I hope they make it to that place. I hope they don't slip and fall. Look at that one. He slipped and fell, and now he bleeds."

He yells out something in MUP speak, and the other MUP laugh. He hands us back our papers. He stares at Alija. She glances sideways. There is an instant of recognition. He doesn't taunt her, and I wonder why. I can see her waiting. I can see her forming MUP syllables in her closed mouth. She is ready for the attack of words, but it doesn't come. The MUP slaps the door and waves us on.

"Be careful," he says. "I hear many bad things are happening."

I roll up the window.

"Drive slowly, Jay. I want to see the faces of those guerrillas."

They are not who she is looking for, but they are the same.

"Did you know that MUP?"

"They're all pigs."

"It looked as if you knew him. He seemed to know you."

"I had seen him somewhere, probably another checkpoint."

"He didn't badger you like usual. It was weird."

"Sometimes you're lucky."

Alija's village is folded between two hills. She hasn't been back since the MUP attack months ago. The houses are flame-blackened and lifeless. The imprints of tank cleats mark fallen courtyard walls; glass is scattered in the road, and two mortar holes have turned the corner of the school into broken pottery. Rocket-propelled grenades made glancing blows to the mosque's minaret, peeling off the alabaster coating but leaving the brick. Dogs root through shops. Water runs through the street. There is the scent of death, but old death, hidden under wooden beams and piles of bricks, death that has lost the sting of pungency. We get out of the Jeep in front of Alija's home. It slants sideways like a Popsicle-stick house that was moved before the glue dried. The roof has collapsed. A bedspread and linens are woven through the branches of a burned tree, and the yard is littered with clothes, utensils, a smashed TV, a battered VCR, mattresses, and family pictures. Possessions have become garbage, and the garbage seeps into the earth, and the pictures have aged and dulled with the weather, and the faces in the pictures are happy, shy, and reticent, but they are slipping from the frames, vanishing.

"Careful before you come inside," says Alija. "It might be booby-trapped."

The hallway wall is leavened with smoke and soot. On this strange black canvas, it looks as if a MUP, using the tip of a knife, etched Saint George slaying the dragon. It's a meticulous drawing; the artist must have had time. Alija stares at it. She spits on the picture and walks on, turning into her bedroom. Her underwear, books, tampons, drawers, rugs, and posters are half ash and half real; just enough to surmise what they are but not enough left to salvage. Her earrings and bracelets are bent and melted. She bends over and puts a ring in her pocket. She runs her hand over the windowsill. Bits of glass sparkle through the grit on her fingertips. She presses two fingers together, drawing blood and tasting it. I am in a girl's room of singed perfumes. What's left of a diary — the silver keyhole and lock shine dully through the ash — rests on a vanity. What boys and thoughts, what chores and duties, what scribbled drawings and secrets were on those pages, now lost? Was it read before it was destroyed? Have enemies with guns stolen her musings and carried them away, forever in their minds, so that one day when they think of all this as old men, the loopy penmanship of a village girl will be on their tongues? Will they speak of it at all, or will they have their own secrets and bury what they've done? Her father's only daughter, Alija had lived in a sanctuary of prolonged childhood. To grow up too fast would have brought village men and dowries and an arranged marriage. She stayed frozen and kept away, for a time anyway, from the MUP at the village boundaries and the suitors in the alleys. This is what I think. I will never ask. We take away what we want from war; we come upon remnants and twist them into beliefs. This room is not Alija's only loss. There is her brother and that other secret. The secret she conjures some nights in bed when she whispers, "Jay, let me tell you my story." Each time there is an altered beginning and fresh nuance, as if cameras placed at different angles had filmed the entire secret and each vantage point is a narrative of its own. I have not heard the ending. I may never know it. My life is asking questions, but part of me desires vagueness, part of me wants comfort in mystery. Let some tales hide in the tall grass, and if they must be known, let them come to me without question. I have chosen people — Alija is one — who will have to close the loophole without my prodding. She turns from the window and looks at Brian and me. Her eyes don't know what they want to say. I think she might break. She doesn't. She turns her back to us. Brian walks down the hall. I put a hand on her shoulder; she lifts a hand to mine, and I feel bits of glass and blood on her fingers. I begin to pull my hand away, but she clasps it hard. She turns and I smell her hair, combed apricot and smoke and well water and the metallic tinge of minerals and trace elements of what origin and purpose I know not, but they all mingle, a quiet metastasizing life in dense black softness. She pulls me to her burned bed, and I feel as if on a playground swing gliding slowly backward from heaven. We lie down and she kisses me. Just once. The bedspread crinkles and turns to ash. I want us to float out of the broken window to someplace else, but there's no magic in me; one day there was, but not now, so we stay, bulky in our coats and half entwined. The sounds in a burned house are different from the sounds in an empty house; they are sharper, but they don't linger as long, they seep into the charred wood and disappear the way the last ripple of an echo disappears in a canyon. I leave Alija on the bed and walk across the hall.

It is a boy's room, a spindly boy's room battered and burned like Alija's. The shattered glass is finer, more glittery, scratching underfoot like new frost on a lake. The mattress is knife-ripped. What did the Serbs find? A treasure, a tin of money, a key to a hidden door? The pictures and posters on the walls, like those in Alija's room, are a scorched collage. Tupac with his grimace and tattoos; a soccer ball arcing toward a goal; a veiled woman in silhouette against a desert oasis; another woman, unveiled, an Albanian pop star, I think, with a diamond stud in her nose, her face alight as if a candle or a projector from an old movie house flickers beneath her skin; Michael Jordan suspended in flight; a vintage Corvette, blue and parked on a beach. The Kosovar flag, with a crudely sewn black eagle, hangs in shreds above the dresser. A boy's room with coiled belts and rumpled socks and Koran pages scattered on the floor near the desk, and shoes: all is marred in the room except three pairs of polished shoes, waiting in the corner. I am like the Serbs, an uninvited guest glimpsing a stranger's intimacies. Ardian? I feel like calling the boy I do not know. Perhaps he'll come crackling over the broken glass, a boy in from the field, bringing in the cold and the scent of horses. I pull a picture of him from the soot. Ardian is in the mountains holding a rifle braced against his thin frame, almost too heavy. Girls have diaries, boys have guns.

"He'd call to me at night when he was little and scared."

Alija walks in behind me; she has left her room and closed her buckled door.

"A dream?"

"The Serbs. Night patrols. They were part of our childhood. Ardian would hop out of bed and come to my room and stand at the window, listening to the trucks and watching the moving lights in the distance. 'They might come tonight,' he'd say. 'Be ready.'"

She walks past me, deeper into her brother's room. She steps into the closet, pushing aside clothes, ashes falling around her. She bends and nudges a piece of wall.

"We knew each others' secrets. This was his hiding place."

She pulls out a bloodstained shirt.

"Remember, I told you that he was beaten by Serb boys a long time ago. This was the shirt he wore that day. He never washed it. He kept it folded in here."

There are other things. A coin from Macedonia, the butt of his first cigarette, a marble, a ring, a tooth, and a picture of him, lithe and fine and smiling, his black hair combed back. He is sitting in a café, his arm draped over a chair, his face bright in the smoke and dim. It is different from the picture of him with a gun. It is the kind of picture a young man takes with him through his life; a picture that captures how a young man sees himself and how he hopes others see him too. A man doesn't get many of those, but this is one of Ardian. Alija tucks it in her pocket. She looks down at the shoes and picks up a black boot.

"He kept his shoes beyond their worth. He polished them every day. When he was a child my father told him, 'Ardian, clean shoes mean a pure heart.' But, Jay, how do you keep shoes clean in these fields and on this dirt? With slush in winter? And in summer rain? But he did, every night. Sometimes, I'd peek through his door and watch him kneel with rags and polish. He'd light a match and warm the polish and soften the shoe. Circular, circular, circular, left then right with the cloth as if he had all night. Then he'd take the brush and shine, then wash his hands."

She runs her hand over the leather.

"Once, after I had had a fight with my mother, Ardian came into my room and looked at me hard and said, 'Alija, polish your shoes.'"

She puts the half-boot down, takes my hand, and leads me out of her brother's room.

"Is there anything we can collect?" asks Brian.

"There's nothing here I want."

We leave the house, stepping over a large bloodstain in the hall. I do not ask. Shadowed dogs gather around the steps, confused over their scorched inheritance. They see that we are not staying and they trot away, noses down and seeking those who may never return. We drive past a felled electrical pole and a split wire snaking slowly over the ground, still crackling and alive. We hit the main road. Intermittent flows of donkey carts and tractors loaded with possessions are leaving the villages. MUP convoys muscle past. Men with guns and pale faces, huddling like hidden tribes, peek out from the canvas shadows of troop trucks. I must be older than I think. Soldiers seem so young these days. Are they men? When I first started in the business, I was as young as those holding guns. I shared their fear and that adventuresome tug of brief insanity that meets the enemy. Senses are never more alive. Staccato breaths, heartbeats echoing through bone, hairline sweat, eyes so alert they water, dry mouth and sweet nervous breath, all in unison, all waiting for the flash and rip, the flit of bullets that warm the air and then the mortars raining down stubby and bright, and the smoke and the ears go numb and speed becomes slow and in the instant you think you're dead, you're alive and you wonder how it can

118

be and you think this will be the last time, yes, the last time you think and you promise this, until the next time the young men with guns appear and invite you to another battle somewhere in the woods.

"Lot of MUP, Jay."

"We may be up here awhile."

"I just hope your sat phone doesn't conk out."

"Don't jinx it."

"I'm going to file something tonight."

"Me too. Time to feed the beast."

"Could be A-1."

I look into the rearview and roll my eyes.

"Okay, A-3, but with a picture. Three-column picture."

"Of?"

"Some quasi-artsy thing. I hope we find this dateman, Jay. Otherwise it's just another shitty war."

The sky is dust gray awaiting pewter; it snows at pewter. We stop at a gas station/restaurant for windshield-wiper fluid. Brian laughs when we see a guy whose hands are smeared with grease and tomato paste.

"Whether it kills me or not, I gotta eat one of this guy's pizzas."

"I could eat."

"Alija?"

"A bag of chips."

Alija gets up and walks toward the guy to put in our order. I see her between a break in the curtain that separates the garage from the kitchen. She and the guy talk close, heads bent. It reminds me of my childhood days in the confessional, whispering sins through a purple scrim and awaiting penance. Alija's working this guy for information just like I worked the priest for forgiveness. You can get anything with the right timbre and strategic pauses. From this short distance, Alija seems to be conspiring with him. But I discern nothing. It's their language. I can't get in unless invited. Alija's smart. I love to watch her work; she pulls, gently, word by slow word, unraveling what's meant to be kept tangled. She's pretty and you want to give her things, you want to see recognition in her eyes that you have unearthed a treasure, offered something of value. She's so young to know this rhythm; part of it is compassion, and part is the hope that somewhere in the sentences is a sound, an inkling, a map to her brother. To Ardian. The young man in the back, like a carrot being skinned, is surrendering to her; he'll tell her more alone than he would with Brian and me sitting there. This guy's serious. No smile. No squint of the eyes. Alija nods her head. She steps through the curtain and sits back down with us.

"Brian, you want fish on your pizza?"

"I never mix the two."

"What's going on?"

"Always business, huh, Jay?"

"Well?"

"The guy and I have the same cousins, once or twice removed. He says the guerrillas come down here at night for gas and supplies. The supplies are hidden in the back. Mostly food, but I saw two boxes of grenades and one box of night-vision goggles. This guy's scared. There's MUP all over the place. His father and some of the village elders told him it is his duty to help the resistance."

"When did it become the resistance?"

"You know what I mean."

"I'd be scared too," says Brian, "if I were selling pepperoni pizzas and night-vision goggles."

"Alija, I know you asked the obvious question."

"Yes. He says he thinks we can come here tonight and wait."

"What do you think?"

"I think they won't talk to us."

"Brian?"

"Success is mostly about showing up."

"Alija, let's go visit this guy's father and make sure it's okay."

The old man is slight, straight shoulders, solid as stone. He offers tea, and we sit on a floor in a big room around a kerosene heater. His wife whisks in with glasses of juice and butter cookies. She doesn't look up. She disappears out the door, and the cool air from the rest of the house rushes in. The old man rolls a cigarette. He looks at us without talking. I'm sure he's thinking, Why don't they go away? Mountain hospitality and his distant relation to Alija prevent him from booting us out. Village elders intrigue me. They rule small worlds legislated by blood ties and ancient oaths. The good ones are calm and methodical. They are gossip and judge, law and order. They understand balance, playing clan grievances off one another and limning justice from adulteries, violated honors, stolen sheep, and other indignities that could splinter a village and jeopardize the land. Life springs from land. Betray the land and you are cursed. Lose the land — even a centimeter — and you are condemned to a punishment worse than hell because you have robbed the unborn and shamed the spirits of those who came and fought before you. The old man leans toward Alija. They whisper. Syllables coil and spark the air. I am a fantastic listener to things I don't understand. They speak awhile, and the old man winces and squints, and his voice goes from somber to light to somber again. They hush. He sips his tea and rolls another cigarette, a flash of thumb and forefinger. He slips the cigarette between his lips and stands, embracing Alija and shaking our hands as he leaves the room.

"Did we piss him off?" says Brian.

"No. He's just a quiet old man. Wants no trouble."

"Well?"

"We have his blessing. He says he will send word to the guerrillas that we will meet them tonight when they come for their weapons."

"And pizza," says Brian.

We wait in greasy darkness amid the tang of tomato sauce. One hour. Two hours. Brian is restless. The road is quiet, and the land is locked down. Scattered MUP units are wedged in bunkers. Helmets rise like dark bubbles from turrets of APCs. The MUP don't like to fight at night. Who does? Only those forced to, only those silhouettes scurrying through fields and black gardens and across pricks of light in far-off windows. I hear them. Distant footfalls are coming quickly toward us. The scruff of dirt and gravel. A light knock. The door opens, and three men with big eyes and Kalashnikovs rush in like a whirlwind born from nothing.

They look at Alija's second cousin. They glance at us. It is a strange party of darting eyes. They raise their guns; their trigger fingers freeze into question marks. Who to shoot first? Alija chatters, and a staccato fury of words erupts. She yells and explains. Her voice cracks for an instant, but she stays strong like the first day I met her in the tent with her stitches and bruises. The old man had assured us this was a done deal. More footsteps scrape outside, and there's another bang at the door. Two other figures enter, one with a twitch and a slightly off-rhythm gait.

"Jay, Jay, Jay. You're turning up in the most wonderful places. Isn't it a lovely night? So much happening. Ah, Jay, things are changing. Hi, Brian. Hi, Alija."

"Vijay, what are you doing here?"

"Stories, Jay, so many stories. I hear things. I listen. I follow. Let's have a sip of brandy. Sssshh. Sssshh. I should be whispering."

Vijay reaches for his flask, and the big-eyed guys lower their guns. The Leopard stands behind Vijay, stroking his impeccably trimmed mustache and peeking out the window. His sidearm is unholstered. He looks to Brian.

"Did you ever get your press pass?"

There is a pause.

Brian smiles, and so does the Leopard.

"We've done much since the last time I saw you," says the Leopard. "Remember the night patrol? We killed three or four MUP, as I recall."

"That's right."

"We've done many more attacks. Our strategy is refining."

"You have help, I hear."

"Jay, Jay, Jay. Always to business with you. Let's have a drink."

The big-eyed guys put down their guns and step into an adjoining room. Alija's cousin vanishes. Blankets are thrown back, and a truck appears outside. The men load boxes and crates of rifles, grenades, night-vision goggles, fatigues, and boots. They are quick, and the only sounds are Vijay sipping his brandy and the creaking of rope handles on the crates. The engine rattles, the men grab their guns and pull down the tarps, and the truck pulls away, disappearing into the black without lights.

"Aren't they worried about a MUP checkpoint?"

"We have sympathizers. War, Jay, has taught me so much about human nature. So many Judases. Money and fear. Fear and money. What great motivators. Very sordid, really. I've become disappointed in human nature. What nasty little creatures we are. I think I shall study that on my fellowship to the John F. Kennedy School in Boston."

"You got in, huh?"

"I'm accepted. I leave this summer for six months in the U.S. I'll have to shut down the paper, I suppose."

"You'll miss all this."

"I'll be back, a mere pause in my evolution."

The Leopard rolls his eyes.

"How do you two guys know one another?"

Before the Leopard answers, Vijay — like an annoying *Jeopardy* player — bleeps in.

"I met Mr. Leopard in grade school before he took on his animal persona. He decided to go into law. He thought he could change the MUP through jurisprudence. The Gandhi approach. Isn't that nice to think? I became like you, Jay. A *journalista*. Isn't that what they call us in Bolivia, or someplace like that? I thought I could change the MUP through words. But we see now there is only one way to change the MUP."

"You always talked a lot, Vijay. Even as a kid," says the Leopard.

"A surfeit of verbal gifts."

"The old village man sent word that you were here waiting," the Leopard says. "We think it's time you came to the mountains. It's moving faster than we thought."

"Is that good?"

"We'll see. We are ready for whatever."

"Jay, what's that saying, 'We have cast our lot'?"

"What's your role, Vijay?"

"I'm a chronicler of events."

"I think something more."

"Ah, Jay, you give me too much credit."

The Leopard opens a map. He flicks on a penlight and traces contours with a knife tip. He is solid. I suspected that from the first time we met. He has made the commitment: freedom or death. It sounds romantic — a bit over the top — but it's the purest thing about war. I'm sure the Leopard's quiet zeal intoxicates the young guerrilla recruits, those waiters and office boys gathered from across the continent who linger in the mountains with knapsacks, guns, and fear. But how does a man find such simplicity when the counterpoint to death is not life but a concept he has only imagined? The Leopard knows nothing of democracy except a handful of pretty words that are supposed to add up to something more than his current predicament.

"I see you have boots."

"You can't win a war without boots."

The knife blade shines over the map.

"We control here and here."

"Why are you telling us this?"

"Frankly, I don't want to. Orders come from higher. You want a story?"

"What's attached?"

"Nothing. Just write."

I didn't need the map to understand the strategy. The guerrillas are trapped in the mountains, staging night attacks and retreating. They need to hold land, but they can't. They're stuck. The MUP don't have many skills, but they have patience and they have perfected the art of torching villages. Hundreds of thousands of families, with their tents, broken tractors, and diseases, are floating, displaced amid the fighting.

"There are other ways."

"Not if you can't hold land."

"The West won't let all our villages burn. There's a limit."

"You may be right. NATO may be your cavalry."

"What?"

"Your savior."

"A Christian word?"

"A euphemism."

"I don't know that one either, but, yes, we think NATO will come. But some of our leaders in the mountains want different things."

"Such as?"

"How far will a man go to free his land?"

"I don't know."

"Maybe you'll see. We have special camps in the mountains."

"For what?"

"We have to move. Let's go. Vijay."

"I'm ready. Brian, give me my flask. We'll crowd into your Jeep, Jay. We head a kilometer up this road. Then left, and you'll feel the land rise, and we'll meet guides to take us the rest of the way. Such a journey we are embarking upon."

"Cut the British affectation. Give me some American."

"Let's roll."

Headlights off. I wrestle with the steering wheel through jerks and bumps on a donkey road. A MUP fire glows in the distance. It's cold. The night makes the landscape a mystery of whispers and goblins. There are no stars; it is snowing, the first flakes I have seen in a year. They soften the sky in broken gray-white gauze. They spin and squall. I love the snow. Unlike the Leopard, I have my freedom, and I seek less honorable counterpoints to death. One is snow. Isn't that ridiculous? I am young when it snows. I am a boy waiting for school to let out early and to be the first to run across the cloaked sidewalk and leave my footprints on uncharted territory. That is special. I could claim a world until the snow accumulated and covered my tracks and a new boy would come and discover something that was once briefly and beautifully mine. Why am I thinking this? Contemplating childhood weather while crammed in a Jeep with a man with a gun, and, beyond the windshield and perhaps beyond the snow, war, patient as an aloof lover, waits in the mountains. Only God is bigger than the mountains. They survive snow and men; they are baritone voices rolling through time.

A light flickers through the snow.

"Stop, stop."

I roll down the window. Snow brushes my face and melts into me.

"Our guides."

"Do we get out?"

"No, we can go farther. This is four-wheel drive, right?"

"Yes."

"Open the back and let them hop in."

"Be careful of the sat phone, Jay," says Brian.

The guides are raw-faced and wet. They climb in, and we move.

"Vijay, why so quiet?"

"Don't you know? A man is allotted so many words a day. I have used all mine."

"I didn't think that possible of you."

"I have my contemplative side."

"I like that side," says Leopard with a laugh.

"It's very appealing," says Alija.

"Ahhh, I am the butt of humor."

"A kind humor."

"If you persist, I feel I will have to borrow some words from tomorrow's allotment and tell you a long story."

"We are done with humor tonight."

"Good. I will drink my brandy in silence."

"How much brandy is in that little flask?"

"I have two flasks."

"Well, give me a sip then."

"I have never tasted alcohol," says the Leopard. "My father was a strict Muslim."

"Have a swig, then."

"No. Why forsake my dead father now?"

One of the guides in the back says something.

"Turn here."

The road worsens, but after a while it smoothes a bit as we switchback our way up the mountain. Snow blows hard and with each turn falls farther into the valley. We are grounded yet flying, soaring through ink flecked with white. The snow illuminates a short distance beyond the hood. The Leopard tells me not to turn on the lights. I keep waiting for the tires to lose their grip on the ice, or for something, I don't know what, to come howling through the blackness and send us over the edge and into the ravine. I can hear Vijay sip. The guides in the back shuffle their boots. The melted snow in their hair is dripping; I see wisps of their winter breath in the rearview. The windows are fogging. My fingertips are stiff, and my feet are cold and tight. I hate it when the feet go. Alija sits between Brian and Vijay. Her eyes are closed, and her head sways. She seems to be dancing, her body given over to the bumps and dips of the road. It is erotic. Strangely, it is erotic.

The Leopard stares through the windshield, studying snowflakes as if they are equations or squiggles to be solved or interpreted. Maybe he's waiting for a bullet; the click-boom of a landmine. He should have a drink. A touch of brandy, warming his tongue and spreading through his bones, would do him good. But he won't drink. Look how pressed and clean his fatigues are. His fingernails are clipped and pure. His father taught him well. The Jeep slides around another bend. A man steps out of the brush. Then another and another and another; so many faces peeking through the falling snow. Hard, smiling, strange, scared, bemused, lonely, angry, uncertain, lost, and bitter faces, they hover before us, an odd family portrait of men. They are young and old, and many are in between. The snow keeps falling, and they stand in it because there's no place else to go. No campfires. Campfires betray. Only the earth will hide you. Know its grooves and patterns. It is indifferent, but it shields. The men have guns, mostly Kalashnikovs, but I see sniper rifles and RPGs. They part as we drive through, peeking into our windows, pressing their faces against us. I will write about a few of them, or those like them. They'll die and be buried in forests and meadows. Their guns will be taken and given to new men, their bullets will be counted and divvied. Their boots will be unlaced and pulled off, and a meticulous man, one with a rifle slung over his own shoulder, will record their deaths in a book whose pages over time will rip and scatter until only memory will be able to retrieve their existence. That is what will happen, but they don't know this now. In the snow, in the mountains, they think they will last forever.

"Welcome to the revolution."

Vijay laughs, and the scents of brandy and wet steel fill the Jeep.

"This is what we control," says the Leopard.

"How many are up here?"

"Thousands in camps across the ridges."

"Where do we go now?" asks Brian.

"We walk." The Leopard opens his door and slides out.

"Where do we sleep?"

"There's a barn and a few caves up a ways."

I don't ask how long we can stay, and the Leopard offers no hint. Vijay disappears with some of the men. He's dipping into tomorrow's word bank. Brian, Alija, and I follow the Leopard up a narrow, crunchy path. The snow has slowed, but the mountain cold grips me.

"Could have been in Fiji, Jay. Snorkeling and drinking in the sun. We're going to have to rig something for the sat phone and computers. I don't see any electricity up here."

"We can charge them off the Jeep engine."

"My little industrious Jay."

"Cold, Alija?"

"Freezing."

"Where are the commanders?"

"Farther up," says the Leopard. "You'll meet some of them tomorrow."

"Will we meet the man with the dates?"

"Don't ask about him. I don't know if it's been decided."

"Have the MUP ever come up here?"

"They sent a recon team once, but so far no attacks."

"Planes? Helicopters?" I ask.

"Nothing. I don't think they've decided what they want to do."

"Everyone should wait until spring," says Brian. "Fighting's miserable enough without doing it while shivering your ass off."

"What if your George Washington had said that?"

"It was always cold back then."

The Leopard stops at an old sheep shed with broken windows.

"You'll stay here tonight. I'm sorry, Alija. It will be very cold."

"I'm numb already. Our sleeping bags should protect us enough."

"What's the name of this fine hotel?" says Brian. "I need to rack up some travel points."

"Alija, what's your brother's name? I'll check to see if he's with us."

"Ardian. He's barely eighteen."

The Leopard turns and leaves.

"I'll send Vijay up."

"Only if he's quiet."

"He will talk you to sleep."

"What do you think, Jay? Would the Jeep be warmer?"

"I don't know. These are mud walls and there's a roof."

"But holes for windows."

"There's no wind. Let's try it."

We slide into our sleeping bags like unfinished butterflies. They are the kind of bags that pull up over your head with a slit for breathing. We're lying next to one another. I think of Ellen. She's zipped in a different bag. Maybe she's back in Philadelphia by now, the dirt fresh around her. How many days has it been? I don't know. I count days by stories filed, and I haven't filed in a while. That is changing.

I close my eyes and see the thing I sometimes see, a woman with a camera, my brief wife, smiling years ago in another forgotten laundry list of gunfire and death. Beirut is nearly rebuilt now. They're grinding bombed buildings into sand to widen the beach near the corniche. Isn't that something? All the ghosts, bullets, and flesh, all the metal, stone, and mortar crushed into fine particles; tons and tons of it, the color of eggshell and chalk, widening and pushing back the shore. Man can be splendid in his audacity. We were out of college and married two years. I, a writer; she, a photographer. We escaped the municipal meetings and car crashes that pad small-town American dailies and packed a couple of duffle bags, scrounged for airfare, and landed in a fifteen-faction-sided civil war between Muslims and Christians and zealots and wackos and the not-so-invisible hand of Israel. We were freelancers in a storm we didn't understand, and we were happy. We made love between battles, and we argued and fought over words and images, so many hours spent on meaning and precision. She liked the words *configuration* and *pigment*. She was a better photographer than I was a writer, and I'd study her pictures, complete quiet narratives of space, dimension, and time, and faces, so many faces hovering on spools and shards of amber-black film. I used her pictures to train my eye. I'd hang them on walls and give myself thirty seconds to describe each one in detail. It was a game. I became a collector of colors and a diarist to the shadowed and bright alchemy of death, birth, and fear, not the overblown and the obvious on the front lines but the barely heard, the ones behind the ones the others followed. My stories began to matter, and one night she said we needed to celebrate, and we found a shack of a restaurant in the sand and ate fish and watched smoke roll over the sea, drinking smuggled wine until we slept. The city fought behind us. The next day she was photographing a battle on a street whose name I no longer remember. The lens narrowed her periphery. One bullet in the neck. She fell in the sunlight near a burning car. I dragged her around a corner. Hands are useless for stopping blood. It trickles through fingers. I tied my shirt around her neck. She didn't cry or seem to have pain. She held on to her camera with both hands. A man helped me carry her through alley smoke and into a house. We laid her on a table. A woman and boy sat in a corner. The woman was dressed for the market, waiting for the midday lull in the fighting. Another man looking like a lunatic but also like a doctor entered. His stethoscope had only one ear piece. He breathed heavily through his nose, loosening my shirt from her neck, tracing the bullet hole with his finger. He closed her eyes. He left the room and returned with a bowl of soapy water. He washed her face and her neck. He called the boy over, and the boy took the camera from her hands and washed her hands and returned the camera, lacing her clean, still fingers around it. We carried her to a taxi, and I held her in the backseat, and we drove to a place where bodies were collected and identified. She went into a bag, like Ellen. But I like to think that some of her is mixed in with the new coastline. That she's a speck in the grand design, a voice in a chorus near the sea. I have little left of her, no letters, no pictures, no scrawl, no line in a book. I carry only her last roll of film. It's too old to be developed. I don't want to see the pictures, anyway. I like the way it feels though, a knot, a bump in my pocket, and sometimes I think I've lost it but it reappears in the bottom of a bag, stuffed into a sock, hidden amid the wires and cables of the sat phone. Her name was Linda. She was her own universe. I've condensed her story down to that. I've edited, but I've stayed true to who she was and what that time was, at least that's what I think, yet I know that editors believe they make stories better, but they only make them different. I open my eyes. Snow blows through the cracked windows but not enough to matter. Is anyone else moving unseen through this frigid night? Rolo, my spook? Milan, my sniper? Ardian? They follow their own maps and knife points. All of us infrared blurs in a scope. The door opens.

"Guys, you awake?"

"What do you think, Vijay?"

"I can't seem to get into my bag. The zipper's jammed."

"Do you have any brandy left?" asks Brian.

"A swallow."

"That swallow's mine if I fix your zipper."

"Brian, you're a hard man. A true opportunist. Done."

"Hey, Vijay, how many guys going to the Kennedy School next year are trying to get into a sleeping bag on a mountain before a war?"

"This is why I am unique, Jay."

The night stays still. Morning is a rough affair. My body feels like a fist that's been clenched for days. The sky is a miserable blue, and there's an orange sheen across the snow. I stand in the broken window and face the sun. I'm glad there's no mirror. Alija shimmies out of her bag and stands beside me. We hear the clink of metal and the murmur of men below.

"Maybe you'll find out about your brother today."

"I didn't sleep all night."

"Be calm. It may take a few days to find him, even if he's up here. There's a lot of mountain he could be in."

"When we were kids my father brought us to this mountain. Not this high up, though. This was our summer mountain. Villagers would come to cool in the heat, and you'd hear all these voices along the streams and the sound of splashing water. It was one of the few places you could go and not see the MUP. My father said it was heaven."

"Did your brother like it?"

"He would run through the stream until he was soaking, and I'd follow. I'd jump on him, and his clothes and his skin were so cool. Our father would build a fire on the bank, and we'd sit until dark and sometimes through the night until morning. My father knew a lot of stories back then. He told them slowly. The flame stayed on his face. Ardian's favorite was one about a mountain lion and a shepherd. The lion sneaked down every night and ate one of the shepherd's sheep. The shepherd tried everything to stop the lion. To trick. To kill him. Nothing worked. Then one night there was only one sheep left. When the lion came, the shepherd hid in the dark. He pleaded with the lion, 'Stop eating my sheep.' The lion said, 'I cannot. I am a lion.' The lion circled and lunged toward the sheep. But the sheep did something very unsheeplike. He spun like a dancer and dodged the lion, who went flying over a cliff and died on the rocks below. The shepherd said to the sheep, 'How did you do that?' The sheep answered: 'I am a sheep, but I watched that lion for many nights. He always pounced the same way. So tonight I stood near the cliff. In thinking only about his hunger, the lion never considered where he might land.'"

Alija pulls tight her coat and leans on me, the sun rising in pieces through the broken window, warming us.

"Ardian speaks English as well as you, right?"

"Better. He had, and I don't know where he got it, a movie almanac. Written in English. He'd walk around blurting out condensed bubbles of English, like the way those little passages are written in the comics. He knows the plot, director, and actors in every movie through 1980. That's the year the almanac stopped. We'd sit around for hours testing him. No one could trip him up."

"What's his favorite movie?"

She doesn't answer.

"I can't believe he might be out here, Jay. With a gun in his hands and a knife in his boot."

"Isn't that what you'd want, though? For him to be part of this?"

"Maybe. But what does he know? He's a pretty boy with a silver cigarette case, a student."

"The Leopard says this war has room for everyone."

"I suppose it does. But I remember the boy in a summer stream." She steps to the broken window and rubs a circle of frost away. "They pushed us into this, Jay. They pushed all those boys in summer streams into war. I hate them for that."

There's a rustle behind us.

"Damn, this is awful. Shit."

"Morning, Brian."

"I'm sleeping in the Jeep tonight, Jay. Look, there's frost on my eyebrows."

We eat bananas, and some men with guns and groggy smiles come and build us a fire in the snow. We make tea. Vijay roams out of the sheep shed like a small, lost bear. He is quiet and sits beside me with his tea, his sleeping bag draped over his shoulders. The sun crests the ridge. Warm and cold struggle around me. The heat from the tea in my hands makes me feel rich. Brian is jittery and wants to file. I have to write, too. We go to the Jeep and pull out our laptops. Alija sits in the sun.

"Write till the battery runs down, then we'll turn on the Jeep and recharge."

"Fiji, Jay. Fiji."

I sit in the front, Brian in the back. Brian's fingers are not supple. He's a keyboard attacker, every stroke a discordant note.

"I guess we write sort of a scene setter, huh? Somewhere in the mountains with the band of rebels type of thing. Nine hundred words, slightly poetic, understated. The coming of war."

"You sound like a movie trailer. You going to talk or write?"

"Just brainstorming."

"We gotta write atmospherics. We haven't interviewed anyone."

"We talked to a lot of guerrillas."

"I mean commanders, strategy."

"Yeah, we need that. Although, Jay, I don't think we're

gonna get a Pentagon-type Power Point with smart-bomb strikes and unfathomable euphemisms."

"Did you cover the Gulf War?"

"I did."

"Did you ever hear so many twisted euphemisms in your life?"

"Yeah, I never knew blowing things up could be so pastoral."

"I like this part of the world better. It's more honest. You don't get shit like, 'We thinned enemy positions and advanced to sector nine achieving our stated goal and further positioning ourselves for victory.' Not with these guys. You get, 'We blew 'em away, burned their village, and raped their grandmothers.'"

"Write. Batteries are running."

We slip into our own worlds. Every writer, even a hack, is master of his page. Moving scenery and people, stoking narrative like you make a fire, stick by stick. Sometimes it's a wheezing, smoky fire; others times it burns incandescent. That's what you're after. Vijay opens the back door and slides in next to Brian. He's got a runny nose and a pen. He starts scrawling.

"Isn't this great? Here we are, three journalists scribbling our dispatches together."

"What are you writing, Vijay?"

"Jottings for a daily journal I run in the paper. Page two with my picture. I'll have one of these men scurry it over to my office later."

"We're using a sat phone."

"Brian, you look so earnest. A diligent schoolboy peering into his computer."

"Quiet, man. I'm past the nut. It's flowing now."

"Brian's writing a scene setter."

"That takes thought."

"What kind of trees are these?" says Brian.

"I don't know. There's some pine."

"I can figure out the pine. I'm talking about the other ones."

"I don't know. Birch?"

"See, that's what I hate. Journalists should have to take a course in botany. Look how many times you're outside and trying to evoke landscape and you have to settle for the generic *trees* because you don't know what they're called. I hate that. I hate not knowing the name of the tree I'm looking at."

"Perhaps you could get a little tree almanac or something to carry with you," says Vijay.

"Don't jerk my chain."

"No, I'm in agreement with you, Brian. Really. We know what kinds of weapons we're looking at. Kalashnikovs. RPGs. Et cetera, et cetera. Why shouldn't we know the trees?"

"Good point."

"And, of course, we'll want to know the kinds of rocks we're looking at, too."

"I don't give a shit about rocks."

The Leopard knocks on my window. I get out, and the two of us walk toward the camp below. Young crimson faces float amid faces of gray-threaded eyebrows and arching wrinkles that mark the distance between son and father. Most of these guys have no boots or fatigues. They seem to have dropped their hoes and scythes and meandered into the woods, hoping someone would gather them into an army. When we arrived last night, they appeared as an ominous, almost infinite band stretching through the darkness. The new day has revealed they are not. There are a few commanders. Discipline is lax, and there is no sustained regime of order. They have plenty of Kalashnikovs. But how many bullets? They have RPGs. But how many rounds? A few old men sit in a circle and draw battle plans in the snow with their canes. The Leopard leads me along the southern rim of the camp. There's a brief shit and piss stink, and we pass through scents of metal and cigarettes and then tea and then, I think, the hint of rubbing alcohol and Mercurochrome, and then damp blankets and fresh-cut wood. But no death. There is no scent of death. Winter stanches the death odor. I ask the Leopard where the dead are. He doesn't answer. We wrestle through brush and onto a path that widens and bends toward a ridge. The sun warms me, and again I feel good. The Leopard moves in quick, precise strides; the snow off his boots sparkles in the sun. His holster jostles. We reach an outcropping. He unzips his coat and hands me binoculars. We take a few steps toward the ridge's edge and then crawl on our bellies and peer through the cracks in the rocks.

"See them?"

"Where?"

"Forty-five degrees to your left, across the ravine in that snow and brown."

"I see. How far?"

"About two kilometers."

"How many?"

"I don't know. They started setting up a week ago."

"Is that a tank?"

"Two tanks and some heavy artillery. We sent a team to scout it. It's guarded too well. We can outflank this one, but if they take more positions like this, it will be difficult. We'll start digging a trench here today and station fifty fighters so we don't get surprised."

We crawl back from the ridge and rest against a fallen tree.

"I know where Alija's brother is."

He tucks the binoculars beneath his coat. He looks at me with his hard Leopard eyes that until today possessed no trace of worry or doubt.

"Is he alive?"

"What I tell you now you can't write."

"Don't do this to me."

"Do we have a deal?"

"How can I make a deal if I don't know what the information is?"

"A deal or not?"

"Will I ever be able to write about it?"

"Yes."

"When?"

"Sooner than we probably both think."

"Does anyone else know what you're going to tell me?"

"Only our leadership and a few others. If you're really asking do any other journalists know, the answer is no."

"Deal."

"There are two wars going on over this land. Us against the MUP and us against ourselves. Both are dangerous, but I am more bothered by the second. The man you speak of is dividing us. He came into our midst as if after a fog had burned away. That's how some of our men describe his coming. He brought money and offered help. He stayed to himself for a while. He set up a small camp with his own men. They are much more disciplined than we are. They traveled light and crossed the border on foot. Soon two hundred of them had arrived. They came from Chechnya. Sudan. Saudi Arabia. Some even came from Berlin and Brussels. It's as if they had been roused from sleep and told it was time to follow the intended path. I can't explain it. Supplies started coming. Weapons. Night-vision goggles. Manuals on strategy and making booby-trap bombs. Then came the religion. He spoke of the Koran the way few here have ever heard. We're not devout Muslims, we're European Muslims. There was no fire in his speech, but his words were pure, and I have to say, although I hate to admit it, intoxicating. I thought we'd find him an enchanting novelty, show him respect and then run him out. The MUP want to paint us as fanatics. What better way for our plight to lose sympathy in the West? But a lot of our men, and, unfortunately, some of our leaders, now support this man. They think he is the only way we can win."

"Why aren't you convinced?"

"He wants to turn our struggle into something larger. But it's not larger. These men just want to farm in peace. I want to practice law in peace. I don't want a bigger purpose. I am not interested in redesigning the world."

"Sounds like he reached in and — "

"He's clever."

"What's his name?"

"They call him only Abu Musab."

"When did he get here?"

"Six months ago."

"Where's he from?"

"Nobody knows. Most say Afghanistan. He says he's a follower of somebody greater."

"A new prophet for Allah?"

"I thought so too, but it's not quite that fanatical. He speaks of another man. He says this man has salvation for all oppressed Muslims. He says this man is a rich man who has forsaken his riches to fight the infidel. He says wars against the unbelievers will rise like blisters across the Earth."

"Blisters across the Earth. Poetic in a purple kind of way."

"Excuse me?"

"Nothing."

The Leopard's sentences are as precise as his footsteps. He had practiced what he was going to tell me. He needs to convince me. Language is a weapon. Nuance. Syllables. They must accumulate in quick or in languid strokes. The lawyer in him knows this. But the Leopard is making his case in a foreign tongue; a misplaced word muddles meaning and opens unintended paths. He is careful, and he tires as he speaks.

"Where's Alija's brother?"

"In a special place."

The Leopard says the dateman's camp is sequestered

from the rebels in a mountain fold above us. His followers built stone and wooden houses and a mosque with no dome or minaret. They dug deep bunkers for weapons. The Leopard says these men are accustomed to the meager and the crude. Women are not allowed. Before arriving at the camp, wrappers are ripped off bars of Lux soap so men will not be tempted by the bare-shouldered model with the uncovered hair. The camp is parsed into divisions. Some of the men form an "intelligence brigade" that fans out on recon patrols and draws battlefield maps of MUP movements. Others belong to the "pious and purity brigade," ensuring the strictest interpretation of the Koran. There are the "military brigade" and the "cooking brigade" and the "instructional brigade" and the "financial brigade" and the "punishment for religious violators brigade." Everything and everyone is placed under a heading and then a subheading.

Under the heading of "intelligence brigade" is the elite unit known as the "holy warriors recruitment brigade." The Leopard cautiously chooses *elite* as if he has not seen this brigade but discerns its existence through musings that have slipped below the cloud line and become fact among the guerrillas. This bothers the Leopard. A man of documents and a collector of evidence in his earlier life as a human-rights lawyer, the Leopard despises the flutter of conjecture. "The MUP," says the Leopard, "are so one-dimensional and easy to hate, why must our revolution turn into something complex?"

It's ingenious, really. The way revolution is produced. You take a charismatic figure like the dateman — I'm guessing he's charismatic; so far I've seen only his picture and, therefore, cannot attest to his charisma — and you create an aura. If he has money, the aura grows. If he has money, an apocalyptic streak, and, most importantly, patience, he exceeds his own mortality. Followers multiply, and mystique hardens, and suddenly, like the Serb farmers listening to the priest in Milan's church, men believe they are battlers in the world's final struggle. How wonderfully egotistical. I am editorializing, and because I have agreed to not yet write what the Leopard is telling me, I am allowed this indulgence as I sit against a fallen tree, my ass wet and frozen in the winter half-light.

"The men in the holy warriors recruitment brigade are all Arabs," continues the Leopard. "They shaved their beards and split into small teams, two or three each, and went to the cities looking for impressionable boys and students. I think these recruiters must be like salesmen. They read human character. It's not easy."

"They found Alija's brother?"

"Yes, they found Ardian studying in the university library."

"And?"

"He is here now, in a special camp up there for suicide bombers."

"You haven't used suicide bombers."

"They're not indoctrinated. It takes time. A young man may say he's willing. He sees his family disgraced. He sees his land occupied. He sees he's studying for a career that doesn't exist for him. In the eyes of his father, he sees that one day his masculinity will be taken, too. This is enough to get him thinking about striking the enemy. But how do you get him to wear the dynamite? How do you get his thumb to press the red trigger?"

"The Palestinians give their bombers religion, respect, money for their families, and the glory of martyrdom."

"This man is promising that and more. His holy war comes with seventy-two virgins awaiting each martyr in paradise. He offers in another world what is forbidden in this one. His gives them sanctity and sex, the cost being their lives."

"Paradise for me would be forty virgins and thirty-two experienced women. Virgins can be tedious all by themselves."

The Leopard smiles.

"How many of these impressionable young men are there?"

"Dozens, I think. The plan is to explode them in Pristina, Belgrade, and other Serb cities."

"You'd lose Western support."

"This man and his followers want conflict with the West. It suits them."

"It destroys you, though. You want me to write about this, don't you?"

"Not now, Jay."

"It's got to be soon. Otherwise, what's the point? The information becomes useless once the first son of a bitch blows up. Can you get me to the dateman?"

"The request is in."

"What about Alija?"

"Don't tell her anything yet. I'm trying to get her brother out. No use worrying her until I know if it's possible or not."

Order is a crazy man's lethal proficiency. The dateman has instilled order on an unruly mountain. The Leopard despises him, but he admires the dateman's rigidity of spirit, something his own guerrillas have yet to attain. It's not about commitment. The guerrillas have that. They will fight. They will be killed. But they are like chalk soaked in dye; the colors penetrate only so deep. The Leopard's men seek comforts. Many of them sneak down the mountain to sleep with their wives and watch TV at night. The dateman's followers crave the hard and the austere. "They seek no earthly future either, I think," says the Leopard. "They are like fuel to be burnt. Joyously burnt. How do you defeat a man who believes he's doing the work of the divine, who believes women wait for him in paradise? How do you kill the vision of a man who has so twisted the Koran?"

"Men have been killing in the name of the divine forever," I say. "It's not unusual."

"This is Europe a breath away from the twenty-first century, Jay."

The Leopard turns for another glimpse through his binoculars at the MUP across the ravine. I remember the first time I heard the peace and musical lyricism in the Koran. It was years ago. I was on a crowded train bound for downtown Cairo. A man rushed in and the doors closed behind him. He slid between passengers and found a place. He opened his Koran, the gold lettering on the cover faded, the pages worn. He recited verse. He was a slight man in an open-collar shirt. He seemed a government clerk or someone like that, a man who worked for low wages but kept an air of respectability with a tie and pressed trousers. His timbre soothed. It set the train's clatter to the rhythm of prayer. The door opened, feet shuffled, a hiss, the creak of metal, and then the doors closed again as the train sped past alleys, crumbling walls, and laundry blowing on rooftops. The man prayed through nine stops. He did not call attention to himself, but his cadences beckoned like whispers in a dream. Passengers around him closed their eyes; in a city of sixteen million they had found repose in a stranger's voice. The desert air was not so hot. The press of flesh and sweat were bearable. All life's annoyances, muffled. The train dipped into a tunnel and the man's voice limned the dark, the prayers not ceasing until the doors opened and he shut his Koran and hurried out with the others toward the stairways to the clamor and the light.

Chapter 12

Clouds race across the half-moon; the sky is ice and aluminum. Brian sleeps in the Jeep. Vijay has wandered off to find a warm place and some old friends amid the guerrillas. The sheep shed is quiet. Alija and I lie side by side in our sleeping bags. Our winter breaths mix with needles of moonlight and floating dust. The mountainside is still. Men with guns slumber and battle plans are crumpled in rucksacks. Tree branches snap like waking spirits. Alija is in silhouette. Then she curls toward me and the words come. I knew they would. "Jay, let me tell you my story." It's my strange, unfinished bedtime secret. Alija, as she likes to do, sets up her vantage points. The story has angles and perspectives. Alija gathers them as if she is measuring and snipping embroidery thread. The story starts with the sound of distant shelling. The echoes grow and shiver like wind across a field. Within minutes, shells are falling in the village. Stone and mud fly. Windows shatter. A cow explodes. (That mental image always stops me for a second.) Patches of fire rise in the dirt streets. Walls collapse. Villagers run. But where? Where is safe? The shelling stops, and the sky is coiled with gray-white smoke. APCs whine in from all directions and set a perimeter with their big guns. The perimeter tightens. Small-arms fire rattles. A helicopter circles. Alija and her parents hide behind their courtyard wall. They hear jeeps and doors opening and footsteps that are quicker and heavier than those of villagers. A woman screams. Two pops from a semi-automatic and she is quiet. Alija peeks through a hole in the wall. Images flit across her narrow view. She fits them like pieces into something whole. She strains to see a little to the left, a little to the right. Then she spots what others in other villages have seen; she had thought it was myth, something invented by the MUP to keep order. Men in black jumpsuits with colored bandanas tied on their arms run through smoke and fire, pulling old women and men from houses and lining them up in the streets. An old man rushes to escape. The men in jumpsuits laugh, count to ten, and chase him. They tackle him and lift back his head. A bowie knife flashes. These bandana men exist, kept in boxes until they are summoned and wound up and released like those muscular toys she had once seen on TV, those toys with snap-on parts and square-jaw faces. How can this be? One of them stops in front of Alija's peephole. His back is to her. It is a broad back, breathing hard. The neck is white and newly shaven and smells of a cologne not sold in the village store. Alija's father lifts a pistol from his blazer. Her mother tells the man to put it away. One gun is not enough. The gun drops in the dirt. All his life he has said he wanted to fight, but he never did and now the time is gone and Alija remembers this so clearly. This is another of her vantage points. She shifts to her father's callused hands and creased face. The pride he took in his blazer; all his promises and strong talk. But what can old men do, really, what can they do except build fires and brush dust from their blazers? She shifts back to her vantage point. The footsteps come closer. They are next door. Alija and her mother glance to the pear tree in the yard. The fruit is small and hard; the money and silver safely buried. Alija's mother takes her hand. She gathers her daughter. She kisses her head and moves her palm down Alija's face and the long hair she had washed in the sink a few hours before. The courtyard door shatters. Two men burst in, their boots keenly polished. Others follow. Alija's father is kicked and punched. A knife is raised to his face, and he is led away. He says nothing. Alija steps in front of her mother. She feels something hard and quick on her face and then another just like it. Her ears go warm inside. She hears nothing. Her legs give, and she falls along the courtyard wall. It is a slow fall, and she counts — or at least it seems she did — sprigs of grass growing amid mud and mortar. She is flat on the earth, black boots moving around her eyes. Another blow strikes. Her mind dims for a moment and then is filled with that long-ago summer dusk when she chased the family's horse across the pasture in a lightning storm. That horse, so fast and scared, trying to run from the sky. How can you run from the sky? Alija remembers this. She was a child. She remembers that horses are beautiful and stupid. When she awakens, she senses she is in her house. She hears boots crunching over broken things. She feels cold. Her clothes are gone. Blood tangs her lips. Her eyes are open, but they don't see much. Everything is squished, like peering through a letterbox or through the plastic they cover windows with in winter. She reaches up to feel her eyes. Her cheeks are thick and soft and sore. She lifts her head. She sees she lies on her kitchen table. A man is between her legs, one of those toy men with the bandanas. His bandana is yellow. There is something inside her. Something she has never felt, like digging in a hollow place she didn't know she had. It hurts. Everything hurts and doesn't hurt. Everything is fast and everything is slow. The mosaic, or picture of the scene around her, is scattered. The digging stops. Another face, another yellow bandana, appears between her legs. The digging starts again, but this time in a different place. There have never been so many men in her kitchen before, not even when the village elders came for tea. Something is different. It is not her kitchen anymore. The pitcher is not there; the vase is shattered; spice tins litter the floor; the curtains are ripped; the refrigerator is open, things are dripping; the teacups are cracked and sharp; the sugar is scattered, and there is no fire in the stove; if this was her kitchen there would be a fire in the stove. Yet it looks like her kitchen. A picture of her father's father hangs on the wall. Her mother's scarf drapes from the chair in the corner. It must be her kitchen. She tries to sit up, but that same hard and quick thing knocks her down. There's the horse again. So stupid, running from the sky. Horses don't know that lightning is God's magic. Her mother told her that, and she will tell the horse if she ever catches him. He is pretty on the horizon, that horse. He gallops, shakes his head, his tail flowing through the rain. Something cool is poured over her face.

The horse disappears. There's another bandana between her legs. Men are laughing, and it seems like a party. Another one stands over her. He is a big, blocky boy, his face too young for stubble. The other men push him toward her. She smells that cologne again, the one not sold in her village. Sweet apples and musk. He kisses her. It hurts. He presses harder and steps back, her blood on his cheek. He stands between her legs. He is frightened. He doesn't want to do what the others have done. She watches him through swollen eyes. She creates a biography for him. He has a girlfriend at home. His mother taught him things. Serbs can be raised well too, she thinks. He is the new one among these men. His bandana has more sheen, the color is more vibrant, like a flower in the field. He is awkward at being rough; a sting of tenderness hides in his kiss. He conceals it from the others. This is what she thinks. Maybe he will not push into her. But this is not so. He is a boy surrounded by men demanding things. Her legs are sore. There is no sensation in the places the strangers have entered, just cool stickiness, like honey in autumn. She thinks part of her body must be hiding, and she is embarrassed that her grandfather's eyes are looking down on her. She never knew him, really. He died when she was young. He left behind stories, two pistols, a box of bullets, and a photograph. All men leave such things. Why is this? On what walls do women hang? She sees a tear in the boy's eye. His face reddens. His bandana sways. He has become one of the others. He pushes harder and harder, and she turns, and through the broken window she sees the horse in the field. He is old. When did he get so old and wobbly? His hooves loose and splintered, his mane knotted with burrs.

He looks at her on the table. What's he thinking? Silly girl, when the sky throws fire, you must run. I ran all those years. You chased me through storms and laughed. But fire never touched me, not when the pasture was green and not when it was fallow. The sky is full of tricks. You must know this. The horse lifts his head and clops away. Alija is turned over on the table. Two men stretch out her arms, another straddles her back. She hears something slide out of leather. Something sharp and slow moves across her shoulder blade. She screams. Her mother's scarf is stuffed into her mouth. It smells of flour and lavender. Laughter rises and fades and then nothing; all is quiet, the black boots and bandanas gone. Alija lies on the table, awake, in a sliver between dream masks and life. The dusk is cool. Gunpowder wisps the air. She sits up and looks out the broken window. The fields glow the way they do in the final minutes of the day. Blackbirds have gathered in the trees along the stream. Their cawing, a petulant choir since her childhood, will soon quiet and they will blend with the night, gliding invisibly beneath the stars, and like snipers they will seek the unlucky and the slow beneath them. The shepherds should be returning home. Maybe they are lost. Where are the shepherds? She reaches back to feel her shoulder. It is bloody and her fingers bump on raised ridges. She traces them, deciphers nothing. She will discover later that her skin, like paper, has been written upon, and the word is *whore*. It is not in Serb but in English, as if the writer had wanted his crude and crooked tattoo to resonate beyond the shrinking geography of his native tongue.

This is where the story usually stops. But tonight there is more. Alija, her voice flat and steady, turns in her sleeping bag and looks toward me in the darkness. I say nothing. She says, "Jay, there is one final thing." I stay quiet, and Alija skins memory and steps further into that day when she sat branded in her kitchen. I close my eyes and go back with her to the quiet house. She steps off the kitchen table and stands. Blood and milk run down her legs. She almost falls. The table catches her. She's cold. Blood is dried and streaked on her breasts. Her fingers curl and attempt to straighten. The house is dim, but she knows its turns and angles. She does not look in the mirror. She wants no light, and she washes nothing. She puts on jeans and a shirt in her bedroom. Mother and father. Gone. She looks out the window. Fires flicker from rooftops. A few bodies are scattered in the road. She knows them. Whoever they are, she knows them. The village is small, a family grown from the same distant seed. The village is not on the map. How did the men in bandanas find it? She wants to sleep. Her bed is prickly with glass and burnt things. She walks down the hall. Someone lies on the floor near the front door. She stops and listens to the breathing, a wet wheeze. It is the reluctant boy with the bright bandana. He sleeps next to a bottle of raki, a knife, and a Kalashnikov. Why is he here? To stand guard? Over what? She sees he has carved Saint George slaying the dragon in her father's wall. Why do Serbs pick this image, as if they are the world's only chosen, as if they are the purest? He doesn't stir, this drunken boy. She sits next to him. He lies on his stomach, drooling like a child, his black boots splayed on the floorboards. His hands are thick and white. He is big, but his face is unfinished and pasty like flour and water before the oven. He lacks lines of time and manhood. He will always be a boy. He was inside her. He pushed like the others. They all pushed. How many? Of all the ones, she thinks she will remember him. She has blurred the others, but not this puffy-faced boy. She straddles him and sits on his back. He doesn't notice. She must be light as a bird's wing. She is hay and dust. She lifts and descends on his breathing. She thinks of the horse she chased and rode home in storms. She holds the boy's knife. It is wide and heavy and balanced. He sleeps. She reaches through his hair like a comb and gently pulls his head back. He doesn't move. She had seen her father do this with sheep. A jab and then quickly across the throat. The boy jerks as if he might awaken, but his eyes stay closed and she holds back his head and blood widens across the floor. She thinks it is red, but the house is dark and she doesn't know. She doesn't hate this boy. Hate is not the only reason to kill. He didn't want to do it, and now he will never do it again. His mother will wail and grieve, but it is better that a boy like this grows no more. Alija releases his head. It slides into the blood; the last breath gurgles like the rattle of a tractor after a long day. She slips off him and lies on her back. She reaches into her pants and between her legs. She wants to pull the last hours out, but she cannot, they are sealed inside her, in those places her mother never told her about and her father demanded she protect. She wipes her hand on the dead boy's shirt; his bones feel like cable. She rises and walks out the door. She digs beneath the pear tree and lifts a sack of money and silver. She steps out the smashed courtyard door and onto the dirt road. Fires lap the night, but they are diminishing. There is little left to burn. She walks past the mosque. The silver minaret is tilted. She thinks of a crooked candle on a cake, or a tree aslant and alone on a plain. She whispers, "Is anybody here?" No answer. Nothing. She leaves the dirt road and heads over the field toward the forest in the mountain crease. Whoever survived went there. She looks for the horse, but he is gone, and she thinks he must have died years ago.

"It's finished, Jay."

She reaches out of her sleeping bag and lays an arm across my chest. She moves closer; her breath cuts a warm hole in the night.

"I understand about the boy."

"I wanted you to know. I sleep with you. I feel your skin. You move over me. But I am not ready for anyone to go inside. Maybe never."

"Do you think about the boy?"

"He is with me, but I don't think about him. He is like the fruit beneath the skin. I took his bandana. I burned it in the forest."

"Do your parents know?"

"I told them everything at the refugee camp. My mother said nothing. She gathered and held me and took me to a doctor. It was okay with her. My father closed me off. To him, I'm what they wrote on my back. I am his blackened daughter. In this culture I don't exist for him. I also killed a MUP, or at least a boy wearing a MUP's clothes. My father only talked about such a thing. I remind him that he is mostly a man of words."

"Your brother doesn't know."

"I haven't seen him. How can he know?"

I don't tell Alija what the Leopard told me about her brother. She kisses me and turns in her sleeping bag. I listen to her small, rhythmic breaths. She moves again, and I hear nothing. It is not close enough to dawn for me to sleep. Rock. Scissors. Paper. Knife. The boy with the lost bandana is dead. A wind moves up the mountain. It rattles and moans through cracks in the rocks. It whistles on the ridge. I can hear it, faintly. I am a night-noise expert. Sounds are the energy of darkness. I count them like beads on a rosary. The rosary lengthens every night. I will add the dead boy. He is a bead I will keep. I knew an altar boy once. He rode a spider bike with cards in the spokes. He had a crew cut and wore a rosary around his neck. We played football together, and before each practice he'd stop at church and say a prayer, his bike parked near the bell tower, his helmet balanced on one handlebar, his cleats on the other. He was fast and hard to catch, but one time we tackled him and his rosary snapped and the beads scattered through a pile of boys in the dirt. It was dusk. I found the cross and handed it to him. He slipped it in his sock and went back to the huddle. The sky was hard and frozen in shades of color. He took the ball again. He cut up the field the same way. We ran toward him in spastic jagged angles, cleats clicking on the hardening earth, but he swiveled left and darted right and he was gone, and when he crossed the end zone he reached into his sock and lifted the cross to his lips. He was the star of our team, the reticent leader of a bony, fast, hard-hitting bunch of boys with too-big helmets and sliding-down pants. Our coach, an electrician, called him the "power booster." The coach gave us all electrical names. If you scored a touchdown, you were a "surge." If you dropped the ball or missed a tackle, you were a "charred fuse." I played safety and was the last "filament" of our defense. I loved that name, so bright and final. I could hang at the edge of the game, a solitary hunter watching a play unfold and picking my target through the blur of jerseys and the clatter of pads. At the end of practice, we'd drink Gatorade and our coach would draw plays in the dust on his car hood. The moon would brighten in the sky. The blood and dirt on our hands and shins would dry in the autumn air, and the kid with the cross would pass me on his bike riding home, and I'd hear the cards in his spokes long after his red reflector faded.

Chapter 13

"Jay. Jay."

One of Rolo's locals whispers at my ear. It's dark. Alija sleeps. The guy must have slipped in with a thread of wind; his breath smells of tea and lamb, and his face hovers over me like a shadowed float in a parade.

"Jay, with me come. Rolo wants."

I unzip the sleeping bag and follow the man out of the sheep shed into stingy moonlight. We head north about one hundred meters and hustle along a path. The man is silent, deliberate, even more precise in his steps than the Leopard. We veer left, brushing through pines and other trees with names unknown. I slip, and the man grabs me. We don't break stride. I feel like a boy darting through the mischief of a broken curfew. Nobody sees us, not the guerrillas and not the dateman's strange army camped in the blue-black above us. I like this feeling. I'm a mote floating undetected through a winter forest. This would be an ideal permanent state. We come to a ridge. My guide disappears.

"You gotta get better boots, Jay, if you're going to play in the reindeer games up here."

I can't see him. The voice comes from behind a rock.

"Hey, Rolo. What's up?"

"What is this, a chance encounter at the corner deli in Charlestown? What do you think is up?" He rises as if he's walking on the night air across the valley, and then he's in front of me, taking shape, that balding pate and stubbly moon face, like some cranky kabuki actor.

"I don't know, Rolo. That's why I'm always glad to see you."

"Have you met him?"

"The dateman? No. We've been camped in a sheep shed for two days waiting for an audience, but nothing."

"One of the plants we had up there was found out. Remember the guy who took the photos I showed you? They chopped the fucker's head off. They videotaped it and sent a copy to his family. We can't get close to this guy. He's impenetrable. His followers are gulping the Kool-Aid, man. By the way, everything I say is off, off the record."

"I've been getting a lot of that. A bit of nastiness must be coming."

"Look out there. What do you see?"

"Infinity."

"Jesus, Jay, you're supposed to be a halfway-decent reporter. Look again. Use these."

"I see two fireflies."

"It's winter, dipshit. Those are cigarettes. MUP cigarettes."

"How far?"

"Maybe three-quarters of a kilometer."

"I think I was on this ridge earlier today."

"You were," he says, then adds: "The MUP are wasting too many villages. Killing too many civilians. The world's getting pissed. I think NATO's coming to the party faster than we thought. Plus our President Clinton has to show he can use his balls for more than diddling an intern in the Oval Office. I wouldn't have screwed her myself. She's too big in the hips, that girl. I like slender hips, Jay. Big breasts, slender hips. That's the woman for me."

"I thought you were more original, Rolo. Thought you'd go more with the rustic, I-only-wash-my-hair-in-rainwater sort of slightly big-assed woman, with a well rifled-through book of Chaucer and fingers pricked from making some kind of folk art."

"Shit, Jay, don't build me a woman. I'm a pretty basic guy. And if I have to listen to some chick misquote someone, I'd rather it be an ancient Greek, or Jim Morrison, or even Saint Augustine."

"How about Goethe? I've always liked Goethe."

"Nah, I mostly stay away from the Germans."

"My desk tells me Washington and Europe are saying there's still time to slip out of this."

"I don't think so."

"Are they going to take out the dateman, too?"

"That's the intel debate. Kill him or let him go and track him to larger things, bigger people. We gotta get to the core of this nest. I vote for letting him go and tailing him."

"You're a bush rat without a tie. Who's listening to you?"

"They listen; sometimes they do listen. I gotta go. Don't want to be around here at first light. I just thought since I was in the vicinity. What's your plan?"

"I've got stories to write. I'll give the dateman a couple days. If I don't get an interview, I'll head back down the mountain and file a bunch of war-is-coming shit."

"Coming fast."

"Yeah, but it plays like a sequel. Or a bookend. Did you ever notice tea is the drink of choice in places where the shit's gone bad?"

"That's why I love you, Jay. You're more cynical than me. Nothing's changed since Troy. The world spins but stays fixed on one point. Annihilation's our destiny. There's no valor anymore, though, that's what gets me. The ancients had valor. Now we just have noise and hate. What crystallizes us as a species? The honor has vanished from the quest, and here we are lapping around in a stew of psychotics peddling their messianic bullshit."

"That's too easy, Rolo."

"I know, but I'm pissed and I'm tired and we're looking at a cloud of big hurt, Jay. It's coming. I've been beating the bushes for years, you know that, but this shit is different. Hey, you know about the dateman's — Jesus, now you have me calling him the dateman — you know about his camps, right? I hope you at least got that far."

"The cleanliness brigade, the suicide bomber platoon, and all the other Byzantine layers of jihad."

"It's like some sinister place in the Catskills where the

strange neighborhood kids go for summer. Kind of bare bones, though. Our satellite images don't show anything major. The guy's still building. Alright, Jay, I'm off. See you in the dust storm."

Rolo jumps over a rock and disappears. His guy with the tea-and-lamb breath leads me back down the path, and then he's gone. I find my way to the sheep shed. A slice of orange muted with slate gray burns far off in the sky. Alija is curled and quiet. I slip into my sleeping bag. I hear footsteps and coughs. The circled stones are cold, but fires will soon burn and water will boil and kettles will blacken. I close my eyes and drift, following cigar smoke and clipped voices to an anteroom. Guys in nice suits with pretty ties. Plum brandy and manicures and some kind of pâté, goose, I suspect. I should have been a diplomatic correspondent. Then I could have waited for war in a hotel or a palace, talked to (diplomatic hacks say "chatted up") officials amid paintings of fox hunts and dead ladies and lords of the manor. I could have been part of the traveling glitter of cuff links, briefcases, secret pouches, varied but refined elocution, and self-generating gravitas. They're ruminating now, a chatter of diplomats and envoys, and, in a high-back chair with golden brocade, President Slobodan Milosevic, with his spoiled-boy's scowl, sits and listens to threats and niceties dreamed up by generals and presidents who are thinking, privately, of course, how crazy is this son of a bitch and how can we buy him off before he starts another mess? They are looking for what they call the "climb down." And Milosevic is thinking, "Ah, look at this parade of messengers from Europe and Washington, flying through the night fog to talk to me, unrolling blueprints for war, drinking my brandy, and then scurrying away like beetles to make their phone calls."

Milosevic likes the pitch of night, eating grilled meat and caviar, throwing little tantrums mixed with the timorous Serb persecution complex and dark Balkan frivolity. He's a nut case with a long cigar. He wanders underground bunkers, accepts money in paper bags. His wife's nuttier than he is. Together, the silver-haired former banker — who, by the way, often seems as if his shoes are too tight or he's suppressing a bout of gas — and his paunchy black witch of a wife with her hummingbird alto preside over a broken toy set of a country. What must it be like to be insanity buttoned in a fifteen-hundred-dollar suit? I can hear the faint thrum now. The ticktock begins. The ticktock is what editors call the big-picture piece. How did we get from point A to point B to point C? It is a shifting narrative to recap what happened. Many will contribute. There will be a file from the Milosevic negotiations, a file from me in the mountains, a file from Washington, a file from some capital in Europe, a file from a village about some poor bastard refugee family. All these will be compressed by somebody on the rewrite desk into one hell of a long story. Probably to run on the Sunday after the calamity begins. I can tell you how it's going to read now; it's so predictable. Except for the dateman. He may add, and I mean this only in a narrative-storytelling-device sense, a refreshing twist. But when it's all over and the peace treaties are signed and the vanquished scurry, what will become of Alija's tale? It will be lost like thousands of others. You can publish only so many stories. The rest are carried and endured and handed down through families until they become a few sentences from another time, or maybe only a single word, like the one carved into Alija's back.

I turn in my sleeping bag. Bits of light gray fill the sheep shed. A map unfolds somewhere, a finger traces. I will have one more drift between waking and sleep before daylight. I wish there was a sandpaper soft enough to rub away the raised word on Alija's skin. In slow circular motions, and blowing away letters made of scar tissue, I could make her pure again. Give her an unblemished canvas to carry into the world. Can you do that, though? Can you take away a stain left by another? I think of that long-ago football field between the school and the creek, the worn grass and the faded chalk lines and the smell of white tape and rubbing alcohol. I see that quick kid with the new cleats and the rosary and wonder if he ever got slow, if he ever broke a leg or wrecked a knee, if he ever had as much fun as those days when he was the most gifted among us.

"Jay."

"What?"

"Why are we never in the place where earth and heaven meet?"

"It's too early for this kind of shit, Vijay. Where's Brian?"

"Writing more atmospherics in the Jeep. I noticed you disappeared the other day with the Leopard. Where did you go?"

"For a walk."

"And you saw things. You heard things."

"Get to the point."

"Alija's brother."

"I know."

"Have you told the poor girl?"

"No."

"What a world, Jay, where young men strap on dynamite and ball bearings."

"You disagree."

"I abhor it. But it may have its place."

"I'm surprised at you. Doesn't sound like the talk of a man on his way to a fellowship at the JFK School of Government at Harvard."

"We are desperate. Imagine the fear one of those exploding men would create in this part of the world. The Middle East, Israel, okay. But here in Europe, what a nefarious novelty. Of course, the IRA and others have been blowing up things for decades. But, Jay, that's different. These men up in that camp have gunpowder and combustible religion. What could be more lethal? What could be more dangerous and exotic?"

"The West cuts you off at the knees."

"Not necessarily. A few explosions and the West pays attention. Understands the tenacity of our cause."

"No. The West would see you as co-opted by lunatics and zealots. Diplomatic condemnation of the MUP would fade. Milosevic would get a free hand. You lose."

"It may be worth the gamble."

"Have you been up there? Have you seen the dateman?"

"No comment, Jay. We are, in of course the broadest

sense, journalistic competitors. Don't worry, though, I haven't written anything. It's not any easy story to decipher, is it?"

"The Leopard's troubled."

"He has been troubled since he was a child. He is a man of reason forced into war. The gun fits uncomfortably in his grip."

"You don't seem to have that problem."

Alija steps into the shed.

"Finally up, huh, Jay?"

Brian follows her.

"I'm deep into another piece. My battery's dead. Show me again how to recharge on the Jeep. I need to do some more interviews, too."

"Sleep well, Brian?"

"Curious people, the Serbs."

"Brian, how's the tree situation? Any new species emerge overnight?"

"Screw you, Vijay. What were you doing rattling around in the dark?"

"I couldn't sleep, and there was no one to talk to. Imagine my predicament. I found a few sentries in a foxhole and we shivered together."

"Sounds like a blast."

"It was, actually. I studied the night. Did you ever really look into the night? See it like a sentry or a night watchman? The night seems liquid to me. It is black, but things run through it, flits of half-formed things. Is there danger? Do you shoot?"

"I didn't hear any shots."

"There were none, just sounds, endless sounds, whispers from the earth."

"There's some atmospherics for you, Brian. Put that in your story."

"The Earth whispered."

"What did it say?"

"Bet on Nightwind in the fourth at Saratoga."

"You Americans are so undeep. Open up to the abstract."

"*Undeep?* I would have expected a *shallow* or *superficial* from you, Vijay."

"I agree with Vijay," says Alija. "Americans joke about everything. You roll in and act as though all will be fixed when you say so. You're fat with confidence. But you don't know this land. It is the night for you, and you don't see all that's in it."

"You mean *you* in a general sense, I hope."

"Yes."

"Pride goes before destruction, and a haughty spirit before a fall."

"Ecclesiastes?"

"Book of Proverbs."

"Not bad, Vijay."

"This is all lovely morning prattle," says Brian. "Point noted, Alija. But I need to charge my battery and write. It's funny, though, huh? Here we are freezing our asses off waiting for an appointment with a guy who in reality wants to kill people like us. He may serve us tea and whack us."

It is suddenly midday. Alija and I interview a few guerrillas, reconstruct their lives to what led them here. I write in the Jeep. Brian pitches snowballs at a tree. Word in camp spreads that the Serbs across the valley, the ones the Leopard and Rolo showed me, are moving forward; there are new foxholes and fresh dirt on the snow. My guess is Milan is close. This is sniper terrain. I'd like to see Milan again. I'd like to cross to the Serb side and hunker for a bit. Milan and Alija, battered by the same land. Milan told me once — I wrote it in a long-ago notebook — about a Serb tale that wound its way through the Bosnian war. It went like this: Muslim paramilitaries swept into a Serb town at night. It was the standard Bosnian massacre, only the ethnicity of victims had changed. In the morning, there were blood and flies and mud and mist. The paramilitaries departed. They left a Serb woman crucified to a barn, her pregnant belly slit, her fetus dangling from its cord. The story became the stone of hate. It spread to Serb villages, and men promised vengeance. Months later, Milan said he met a man from the massacred village. He asked him about the woman. The man told him the woman was his wife. Milan cried and bought the man a whiskey. He hugged the man, and they ate dinner and drank until dawn. The man stood to leave. He leaned his forehead into Milan's. There was a woman, he said, but she was not his wife. She had been killed, but not crucified. There was no barn. She was barren. Yes, the man said, he was from the village. He heard the massacre while hiding behind a rock on a hill. It went on for hours. He was the village's sole survivor, and he invented the crucifixion story. Why? The man said massacres and village burnings had become common. They numbed and deadened but did not anymore inspire vengeance. They no longer shocked. "People needed some-thing more," said the man. "I gave them that. They believed in that story more than they believed in God. It became their God." Other such stories were told and retold, fictions loosed like rain upon the land. Villages were haunted. Villages were cursed. Villages were emptied. Children and mothers disappeared into the maw, and men slunk into the hills. Life frozen the way a camera catches a moment. A teacher's assignment left scrawled on a chalkboard, a carton of milk on a grocery counter, a dead donkey tethered to a hitching post, the long ash of a cigarette left by someone in a hurry, the running of water, the peaches rotting in the or-chard, the wheat left too long in the fields, laundry billow-ing on lines like fading flags. The people turned invisible, slipped into the air like a coin in a magician's hand. Ghostly villages turned into props for narratives. Milan said he in-vented stories, too. He kept them to himself. Each burned village he traveled through had a fairytale. Not the castle kind. The castle kinds were over. They were simple. A woman peeking through a curtain, the scruff of a soccer ball in the dirt, a girl in a new dress, dust on patent-leather shoes, Easter lamb, long bottles of raki, a table of cakes, a wedding an-nouncement, a dance in the field. I told Milan they weren't fairytales. They were life.

"Whose life?" he said.

Where is Milan now?

The Leopard knocks on the Jeep window.

"No decision on when the dateman will see you."

"It's not going to happen, is it?"

"I don't know, Jay."

"Alija's brother?"

"Nothing yet. Maybe you should go down the mountain for a few days and then return."

"Can we get back?"

"Go to the same man at the gas station. We'll meet you again."

Chapter 14

"The dateman's overrated, Jay. Probably doesn't even exist."

"He's there."

"Screw 'im."

"Turn here," says Alija.

"You sure?"

"This is the way."

The snow has turned to slush. We are driving in a valley; the mountaintop to our back is lost in fog and sleet.

"What now?"

"We seem to have run out of atmospherics."

"Screw you too, Vijay."

"Brian is an angry boy today. I must buy him a tree book."

"Anybody have alcohol?"

"Fanta."

"I hate Fanta. It's not a real-world drink. Who drinks Fanta in civilization?"

"We'll see the dateman, Brian."

"You've probably already seen him, Vijay. The way you ferret and sneak around up there in the woods and dark."

"I have not talked to him. But I can tell you I have been close. I was up there, a door opened, and I glimpsed him. The door closed. He did not want to see me. He is real."

"Slow down," yells Alija.

A tree lies across the road. I brake and swerve. We sideswipe it and jerk to a stop. Seven men rush the Jeep. They open the doors and yank us out. We all get a muzzle in the face. These guys aren't from here. They're bearded and lean, stringy like jerky. There's no talking to their eyes. Black boots. Green fatigues. Two of them have long scarves laced through their hair. I hear the throaty consonants of Arabic. Hand motions. One of them hops into the Jeep and searches our bags. I'm thinking good-bye sat phone, but the guy doesn't touch it. He hops out with a bunch of handwritten pages. He holds them up to the others and runs toward the woods.

There is a silence between rustle and scrape, and the man with the papers vanishes into the brush. The others, guns cocked, retract slowly. One of them turns toward Vijay. A pop. Vijay goes down. The bearded men disappear before the sound of the shot fades; the last I see of them is two scarves, one blue, one green, coloring the fog like kite tails. The bullet struck Vijay in the temple and veered out his forehead. His left eye is gone. Brian kneels and holds Vijay's skull together. His hands turn red. Vijay is alive. His one eye darts and rolls as if knocked from orbit. He gurgles air. He wets his pants. He is like a half-finished painting, blood, a smattering of teeth, skin turning the hue of birch. I bend toward him. Alija takes his hand.

"We've got to lift him into the Jeep."

"He's losing too much blood," says Brian. "I can't stop it. Alija, grab a shirt or something from the bags. He's going to bleed out before we get him anywhere."

Vijay lifts his right arm.

"His skull is too shattered. I can't keep it in place."

Vijay's words, all his syllables and inflections, leak away.

"Vijay, can you hear me?"

He cannot. He has a pulse, but barely; it is like a faint stream of water through a garden hose after the spigot is turned off.

Alija throws Brian a T-shirt. He wraps Vijay's head. Alija takes his hand again.

"His fingers are cold."

Death starts from far away. A tribesman in Africa once told me death is a stranger heading toward a house; sometimes he moves quickly, sometimes he meanders. The heart is home. He comes to the heart last, after he has frozen the rest. Alija whispers to Vijay. She tells him he once danced with a countess and ate calamari. It was on the Croatian coast. She tells him he was poetic and wonderful, a true character. She doesn't tell him to breathe, or stay awake, or hold on. She offers no lie. She gives no prayer. She holds his cold hand, feels the blood recede, tissue compress. She leans close to him, her hair brushing his dying face as it has brushed my skin on so many nights. Brian is soaked in blood. He is crying but doesn't know it. Vijay's head is in his lap. The Jeep's doors are open, and I hear the ping-ping-ping sound of keys left in the ignition. There is drizzle but no wind. The trees in the forest creak. It's strange not to hear voices, to be four people without words.

We lay Vijay on the backseat. Brian sits with him. I back up from the fallen tree and find another road. It's almost night when we locate a village and a clinic run by Doctors Without Borders.

"Put him there on the table."

"We have to call his family."

"Alija, who are his family?"

"I don't know."

"We'll call his newspaper."

"I can have one of our staff take the body into town in an ambulance."

Megan. How strong you sound. That flat midwestern accent is so full of assurance and measured tenderness. Your rubber gloves are tight. Blood swirls on them like finger paint. Look how you trace death, from the abdomen to the chest to the yellow-blue face to the skull to the blood-black hair. So slow you move over this quiet terrain; the body is a rainbow of deep color. Flecks of gray, magenta, glints of shattered bone small as baby teeth. You pick them up with so much science in your glance.

"The bullet exited here."

"Don't put him in a bag."

"What?"

"I don't want him zipped in a bag."

"Jay . . ."

"Put him in a wooden coffin. There's plenty around."

"All right."

"We'd been driving for miles, and then I turned the bend and saw your clinic light. When did you get here?"

"After our night at the bar in Pristina."

"You're close to the mountains."

"So far we're only tending to car accidents and tractor crashes of refugees. There's that strange silence out there."

"I know, but it's not silence. It's like the murmur of beetles in the heat."

"You want to get cleaned up? We have hot water."

Brian, Alija, and I take turns showering. We burn our bloody clothes in a metal drum and drink raki. Megan joins us. Snow falls but melts over the arc of our flame. Four men carry a coffin into the house. It is borrowed from a mosque and stained from deaths past. Coffins here are not buried; they are vessels to the grave's rim. The body enters the earth wrapped in linen. I hear the lid open. The breaths of men lifting. The coffin hurries through the night, illuminated in the red taillights of the truck. There is a bang, the click of ignition, the whine of an engine in reverse, the tires on the main road, headlights on, the rattle of gear change, and then the snow becomes the only color in the night.

"I'm going to sleep," says Brian.

"How you doing?"

He doesn't answer.

"I'm tired too," says Alija. "I think I've gotten all of his blood out of my hair. They'll bury him tomorrow."

I stay and sit with Megan in the snow by the fire. A man comes out of the house and hands me a sack. Vijay's wallet, a few pens, a little money, a map drawn by Vijay, business cards, a bullet, a comb, a mint, and a folded piece of paper with the letter R written above a sat-phone number.

"Have we ever danced?"

"I don't know, Jay. We've done a lot of things."

"I think we did dance."

"Maybe."

I throw sticks in the can. The fire brightens.

"Who was your friend?"

"A local hack on his way to America."

"What's happening up there?"

"The planning of two wars."

I move closer to Megan. She smells of oranges, blood, and smoke. Her hair is pulled back. It fights the rubber band in the way thick hair does, and strands of it float untamed in the firelight. She has her chin on her knees. The lines around her eyes are thin, as if drawn with a needle. She could not heal tonight. We brought her something she could not fix, like a stillborn calf from her childhood on her father's farm. All she could offer was the exact place of the exit wound. She dabbed Vijay's face with cotton, pinned his name to his shirt, and sent him on his way. People are deliberate and clipped around death. They are the way the Leopard moves through the forest: methodical and waiting for it to be over.

"I didn't think I'd see you so soon after Pristina."

"Pristina was nice, Jay."

"It was. I'm out of shape."

"You look fine."

"No, I've got to start jogging or something."

"I don't think they do much jogging around here."

"Take your stethoscope and listen to my heart."

"Jay."

"Really."

"Lift up your shirt."

The stethoscope glints like a coin.

"Sounds like a bell, a nice echo. You're fine. Are you trying to stay young for that translator of yours? That's not like you, Jay."

"I'm an old lady's man. The young need too much instruction."

"They are nice to look at."

Megan and I go inside. A candle burns on the table. We lie on separate couches. I would like to go to her, to lie beside her, but I don't. It is enough to hear her breathe. A guard patrols outside. By now, Vijay's passed through the checkpoints and is in Pristina. They'll cut off his clothes and wash him. Women will gather, and men will go out at first light and break the frost line to the soft earth. The grave will widen. Vijay will be carried through the snow and lowered into the dirt. People will whisper that war is insatiable, unfolding through mountains and creeping across valleys, taking the best and the worst, indiscriminately. They will hate the Serbs, as if they could hate them any more, for a death committed by another. Vijay, the new martyr, his picture photocopied and hung, his black eyes peering through streets and alleys, blowing in the wind, ripping and fading until he is diminished and all that's left are staples and faded strips of paper. Then a new face will be hung. And another. And another. This is what I think, but what do I know about anything? I get up and go outside. The guard waves. I put the sat phone on the hood of the Jeep. I dial the number on Vijay's paper. There is that gap, that fuzzy pause between connections. It rings.

"Yeah."

"It's Jay. We need to talk."

Rolo sits in the bones of a house in the woods beyond a stream. He lives easily amid charred things. He moves through another's heartbreak, he borrows their forks and cups, eats the rice they've left behind. He is a refugee himself, a man with a bag of electronics and a map in a game of someone else's creation. That's the beauty. To be dropped in and to secretly skitter across this terrain and then vanish, leaving nothing and taking nothing, except maybe a trinket from a house just to remind yourself that one day you were making mischief in the mountains. A man like Rolo can change everything, though. A poorly rolled cigarette dangles from his lips.

"Jay, our little chats are too frequent."

"This is a small place. You look tired."

"You called."

"Vijay's dead."

"I figured."

"How long?"

"We recruited him about a year ago. He was perfect. He knew everyone. He was coy and flamboyant. He could move between all the worlds here. He was a journalist, so his asking questions didn't raise suspicion."

"Why did he agree?"

"He wanted America. We promised him that fellowship he kept yakking about. Do us a favor, we do you a favor. He loved it. You know what kind of guy he was. You know he loved it."

"Now he's dead."

"All we wanted was some basic intel from the mountains and some longitude and latitude coordinates to lay down a bombing grid if things got that far."

"What happened? How was he found out?"

"I don't know, Jay, I really don't. This guy up there, your dateman, we just can't get to the bastard."

"The guys who killed Vijay spoke Arabic."

"Remember the movie *Alien*? Something from the outside comes inside and turns nasty."

"Jesus, Rolo, you're going to have to do better than that."

"I know, but I'm tired."

"We were with him. Why didn't they kill us?"

"Probably figured why agitate Washington. They're not ready for that yet. These are calculating Allah's boys, Jay. They're not foolish. They're more mathematical than emotional. "

"You don't seem talkative. I'll let you be. I just wanted you to know."

"Nothing personal. Just frustrated. You know how Vijay never could shut up. He was like an always-running faucet. I asked him once about what he thought was going on up in the mountains, and, get this, he quotes Oscar Wilde: 'The worst vice of a fanatic is his sincerity.' You going to his funeral?"

"No, there's too much going on."

"A true friend."

"There are no true friends, Rolo, just guys you pass on your way to someplace else."

"Stay out of the Hallmark business."

"Noted."

"Jay, one day you'll come to Boston and I'll take you on my father's old bus route. We'll get drunk in all his old taverns like I did when I was a kid. My mom used to make me shadow him to make sure he got home and didn't fall into the Charles. She said she'd be mortified if she had to fish him out of the river and wake him at St. Jude's with everyone tsk-tsking and knowing."

"I think we'll meet in other shit holes before we get to Boston."

"The way the world's going."

I leave Rolo and head to the Doctors Without Borders house. The guard waves at me. I slip in and go to Alija's room. She sits on a mattress, rows of gumdrops at her knees, her damp hair hanging. She says she's worried she'll run out of gumdrops; there are fewer places to get them now that war is coming. She says she won't have anything to give the children we meet. I tell her that we'll give them coins. I have a bag full of coins. She says gumdrops would be better to give in war. She lies down and faces the wall. I ask her if she wants me to stay and she says no. She says it's funny that we now say war is coming, when war has been here for so long. A tear is swallowed. She pulls her knees to her chin, retracting even from the speck of space the world has granted her. I go back to my couch before Megan wakes. Her breaths a ticking clock; her hands scrubbed and white, knuckles chapped. There are scalpels and sutures in a cabinet, rolls of gauze and bandages, antibiotics and morphine, enough, maybe, to keep the dying alive a little longer.

An hour passes, then another. Alija stirs in her room and then walks through the hallway and steps outside into a morning of low clouds, a creak of yellow and blue in the cold distance. I get up and watch her from the window. Another door opens, and Brian walks outside. He and Alija stand near the Jeep. She picks at the ice on the windshield; he leans on the fender. Brian lights a cigarette and hands one to Alija. I have never seen them smoke before. The guard comes over, and he smokes too. They are like workers on a factory break, standing in the chill, free from machines and din. The guard says something. Alija smiles. She translates for Brian. A man arrives in a truck and hauls boxes into a shed. Another guard comes, and the smoking guard says good-bye and walks down the dirt road, his rifle riding loose and low off his shoulder. I hear Megan behind me, and then I see her outside. Brian hands her a cigarette, and she smokes. They talk for a while. I hear shreds of this and that. Alija touches Megan's face, the way girls do when they're young and practicing with makeup. Alija takes a brush from her coat and brushes Megan's hair. Brian lights another cigarette. The man who was loading boxes brings them tea and sugar cubes and puts bread and cheese on the Jeep hood. He smiles and has the muffled chuckle of a man taught long ago by his wife not to wake sleeping children. I hear spoons clinking in tea. I hear ice crack. I hear the wood of the house expand. I think I hear the brush go through Megan's hair, but that is only a remembered sound. Megan stands. She is pretty and smooth and she whirls toward Brian and they play dance and Alija and the guard laugh and the man who brought cheese turns on the radio in the Jeep. Brian tosses sugar cubes in the air and catches them in his mouth. The guard tries, but they bounce off his forehead or miss him altogether. Alija brushes her own hair, long strokes, first the outside, then the thicket beneath. A quiet ambulance comes up the drive. The two men who took Vijay away get out and open the back doors. They slide out an empty wooden coffin. They lean it upright on the shed and remove the lid. One of them goes into the shed and brings out a hose. It is cold and the water doesn't flow at first, but then it does and the man hoses out the coffin and the other man pats it with a towel. They point it toward the sky, but the clouds are a vise and the sun is the width of a penny. Brian looks at them and tosses his cigarette into the dirt and walks away. The teacups are removed from the Jeep. Megan twists her hair into a rubber band; she reminds me of the young Megan I first met years ago, the one with the new doctor's bag and iodine stains on her fingers. Megan, how long has it been? You are my ghost, my echo of wars gone by.

Alija walks to the coffin and rubs her palm over the inside. She says something to the men, and they point to the top of the coffin. Alija gives them each a gumdrop and then walks to Megan, and they both come toward the house. The man with the cheese and tea disappears; the guard walks his rounds, stopping at the Jeep, turning off the music.

Brian writes. Megan counts needles. Alija takes another shower. I hook up the sat phone and check my e-mail. My desk informs me negotiations with Milosevic are failing. The Europeans are squawking about "peaceful resolution," but Washington is pressuring and refugees are streaming. Factor diplomacy into an equation of morals, history, and global stability and then divide it by momentum, and the answer is simple: Milosevic has to go. NATO bombing, writes my desk, seems "imminent." What an ominous word *imminent* is, blows up your spine like wind. Editor testosterone levels are rising. I can see them chattering in their meetings and fixing grand schemes with ink and graphics. It's easy to be tough when you're not in the place where the bombs drop.

I'll soon get that call from the top editor. It's the lawyer-cover-your-ass-from-liability call and it'll go something like this: "Jay, we appreciate the sacrifice you're making, uh, hold on, I'm headed into a tunnel, these damn cell phones. Jay, you there? As I said, we know how hard it is for you, and if you want to get out, we understand. No story is worth a life. Are you married, Jay? Hang on. I gotta make a turn, gotta switch the phone. I'm back, okay, as I was saying, have you got a flak jacket, Jay? You gotta have a flak jacket. But if you want to leave it's still okay. Your safety's the main thing." At this moment, and I've imagined it often, I'd like to tell the editor: "You know what, you're right. No story is worth a life. I'm coming home. Thanks a lot for caring." There would be a long silence, not because of a tunnel, but because the editor would be so stunned to hear of my imminent departure — there goes his dateline from the war zone; how will he explain it to the guys at the club? — that the phone would slip out of his hand and thump in his lap with the accuracy of a cruise missile. But I won't say that. I'm not bitter. This is the way things are. I tell Brian about my imaginary answer, and he can't stop laughing. "That would be so cool, wouldn't it? 'I'm coming home.' Could you see his expression? In my case, though, Jay, I'd have to say I'd not be going home but to Fiji."

"What is it with you and this Fiji fixation?"

"I'll tell you," says Brian. "When I was a kid they thought I had this strange disease. Some weird non–life-threatening thing. I can't even remember the name of it now. Anyway, once a week for four weeks I'd have to go to the clinic and have blood taken, and there was this poster of Fiji on the wall. A tanned girl with a lei and a coconut or something and a beach, and I'd just stare at it as my blood ran into a vial."

"Sounds like some prepubescent sexual thing. I don't want to hear any more."

"C'mon, Jay, I'm just explaining Fiji."

"I was thinking about going with you, but now, no way."

"You wanna go, Megan?"

"Would I have to wear a lei?"

Alija walks into the room.

"We have to go back to the mountains. I need to find Ardian."

I still have not told Alija about her brother. There has been no right moment. I hope in the two days since we've left the mountains that the Leopard has plucked him from the ranks of martyrs playing with dynamite and religion in the dateman's camp of promised virgins. What is it about spirituality and the unspoiled woman? Why does so much intersect there? The air, the land, the seas have all been fouled. We spin in vile matter. Man himself was born muddied. Perhaps woman, with her thin membrane, that onionskin between goodness and sin, is our innate hope for purity. Or is she the rib pulled from Adam, the clay and marrow of a darker place? Vijay would say she is both: temptation and virtue moving through chaos. But why arch into the dense calligraphy of philosophy and piousness? Let's keep it tabloid simple. Zealots play with meanings and reduce them to instinct: man's need to get laid wrestles with his inability to accept his true nature. He falsifies purity and destroys what he cannot change; the world spins on this splendid irony. Virgins are the reward.

The Leopard told me that the suicide bombs in the dateman's camp are refashioned life vests stolen from airplanes. Dynamite replaces the foam of survival. We blow up what we once floated upon. Such details make a reporter's notebook happy. But they don't answer my question. Why haven't I told Alija about her brother? Why do I always say *brother*? His name is Ardian. It's true that I don't want to hand her more despair. She has been raped and written upon; she dug the family silver from the earth. Perhaps it's something more, though. Maybe I'd lose Alija. Maybe she'd break and never come back. I'd be on the brink of war without a translator. Language and nuance gone. I sleep with Alija. I count her secrets, but can I say that her interests outweigh mine? Aren't our interests really the same in the end? Is she better off knowing that her brother's in a place she cannot save him from anyway? Who keeps the scale on how our needs and whims bleed into another's? The same knowledge that creates compassion is the seed of selfishness. So we dance, with one another and around one another. War, however, mocks such abstractions. War is dirt and blood, the elements. It is, as a marine once told me, "Something you can get your mind around 'cause if ya don't you'll get your ass blown off, sir."

We load the Jeep.

"I'll see you again, Jay," says Megan as we leave her clinic.

"Somewhere."

She wants to say something else, but she doesn't. I see her waving in the rearview; then we hit the main road and accelerate toward the mountains, and she is gone.

"Back into the breach, dear friends," says Brian, his voice flat and unconvincing.

The shit comes fast. We meet the Leopard's guides at the assigned place, but the fighting is heavy between the MUP and the guerrillas. The MUP have tightened the perimeter around the west end of a mountain and are firing the big guns. The guerrillas scramble over paths and hidden roads. Their knowledge of the terrain is saving them, but soon the sieve will tighten and they will be eclipsed by the MUP's firepower. We watch with binoculars from a kilometer away. Blasts of flames and white smoke. The blackbirds are circling; there's no place to land. Snow falls in a light fog. Teams of guerrillas, trying to get closer with their RPGs, flank the MUP from the east. A MUP unit peels away from their artillery and starts lighting up the guerrillas. The guerrillas slither into the thicket and try to take cover in the ruins of a village. The MUP cut them off, and the guerrillas spin north and disappear. The MUP regroup at the artillery. Two tanks burst out of earthen bunkers and head toward the village. An RPG streams from a ditch and hits one tank. The tank keeps rolling. Another RPG whooshes past the tank and slams into a tree.

"The guerrillas don't have much ammo," says Brian.

"Hardly any counterfire."

"Jay, get me up that mountain," says Alija.

"We have to wait."

"There'll be places to get up later," says Brian. "We're only seeing one slice of this. The MUP won't move at night. They'll hunker."

"Jay, what do you want to do?"

"One of us stays here and finds some guerilla commander. The other goes to wherever the MUP camp is. Then we'll pool it."

"The MUP aren't going to say shit, Jay. They'll shoot first."

"You and Alija stay here. Call the Leopard on the sat phone. I'll take the Jeep out to the main road and see how far I can get."

"Translator, Jay, translator. You know about eleven Serb words and several of them deal with 'Where's the booze?'"

"Some MUP speak English. I'll see if I get lucky. We need some assessment from the other side. Maybe I'll run into some Serb hacks. They speak English."

"Don't be gone long."

"I don't think the fighting will swing in this direction."

"Alija, are you okay with this?"

"Yeah, Jay, but we get up the mountain, right?"

"That's the plan."

The MUP camp is muddy and crisscrossed with APC and tank treads. A blue-eyed officer, possibly the biggest, broadest man I have ever seen, marches toward the barbed wire at the checkpoint and grabs my passport and MUP press pass. The MUP hate reporters, and the press pass is another of Milosevic's false veneers to create the impression that, despite Western propaganda, he is committed to democracy. There are thousands of little, scruffy men in shiny suits bent over laminating machines across the country spinning out press passes and credentials in a Balkan jungle of manila folders and rubber stamps.

"An American?"

"Yes."

"Americans I don't like these days. Wait here."

He is one big man. The snow whirls around him. He takes my passport and press pass into a shack. I stand in the mud. Mud is very much the same throughout the world. A young guard standing a few feet away asks me for a cigarette. I tell him I don't smoke, and we both listen to the firefight and the distant percussion of artillery.

"Have you seen the battle?"

"I drove past it."

"I'm going up tonight."

"Your English is good."

"School and TV. I was studying languages at university but got drafted."

"How long?"

"They said one year, or until I die." He laughs. "I wish you smoked," he says.

The kid is lanky, a spackling of fading acne on his right cheek. He is pale in his blue-gray fatigues. "How long have you been here?" he says.

"A few months."

"It's a shitty place. We should just give it to them."

"I thought this was holy ground to the Serbs. Field of the Blackbirds."

"Field of nothing. What's America like?"

"I haven't lived there in a while."

"Kids?"

"No."

"Wife?"

"No."

"Just like me."

"Basically."

"You think NATO's coming?"

"Possibly."

"I hear the bombs dropped by NATO planes are so big that pebbles dance off the ground when they hit. I think guys like me on both sides are going to get wasted. A guy in our unit got it the other day. He was talking and then he wasn't. You ever drag a dead body? Heavy, like dragging a bag of chains."

"Have you lost a lot of guys?"

"He's the only one I saw. But no one's gone into the fields to collect what's fallen."

"Have you ever been to the Adriatic?"

"Before the first war. My father used to take us for the summer. He had a boat."

"I hear the calamari is good."

"The best. The Italians think they have the best calamari, but no way. They don't even have the best prosciutto. That's in Montenegro."

"Serbs are good with meat. Best hamburger I ever had was in Pale, you know, just outside Sarajevo."

"Nah, the best hamburgers are in Belgrade at this little place near the river. You can just sit there in the sun, eating hamburgers and watching girls. What do you think of Serb women?"

"I like them, but too much tinted hair."

"I think the chicks down here are sexy. I like darker skin."

"I didn't think you were allowed out to see women."

"We're not. I see them when we're driving through villages. They walk arm-in-arm in twos and threes. Some wear head scarves, but most don't. It's so dirty here, but they look clean, as if they've figured out a way to float through the dust without it sticking to them. They hate us, but they don't show it. Sometimes I feel like shouting to them, 'Hey, I don't care if you keep this fucking land.'"

"Have you killed anyone?"

"Shot into the trees once. Probably only wasted some berries and leaves. I don't really want to kill anyone. I don't hate these people. They're just keeping me from doing what I want to be doing. You're not going to put any of this in your paper, are you?"

"You don't want me to?"

"I guess I don't really care."

The big guy with my passport comes out of the shack and walks toward us.

"See you around," says the guard. "Next time bring cigarettes."

He walks away. The big guy tells me the commander's not here and there's no one authorized to give information. *Authorized* is a popular concept here, and even the roughest Serb grunt can pronounce a crystalline *not authorized* in English. He hands me my passport and press pass and orders me to leave. He tells me I could be a spy. He says Americans have many spies in these mountains. He says America watches him by satellite while he sleeps and counts his troops with a big computer in the sky. He says he'd like to shoot me, but he doesn't have the authority. I try to joke with him and tell him I am glad he doesn't have the authority, but this, I can see, only makes him want to shoot me more.

"Do you know Milan?"

"I know many Milans."

I give him Milan's last name.

"The sniper?"

"He's a friend."

He narrows his eyes and nearly grins.

"You have a sat phone? I use your sat phone, then I get you Milan."

The big guy dials a number in Belgrade. He mumbles for a while, and then his voice goes high and strange. His words stretch out. He sings Serb nursery rhymes into the phone. There is a pause, and he cups his hands around the receiver, trying to block out the war rumble. An explosion rocks the ravine, a firefight follows and then dies. He looks toward the mountains and sings another lullaby to a distant, frightened child. He whispers into his hands, this big man standing in the sleet and mud. You could draw the map of the world on his back and still have space for another ocean. He laughs and makes kissing noises into the phone. There is a pause as if a word failed to swivel through the air and technology to him. His face tightens. His voice goes normal. He uncups his hands, mumbling into the receiver for another minute. He rolls his eyes and hangs up. The screen on the sat phone says the call lasted six minutes, forty-nine seconds.

"Let's get Milan," he says.

The camp is not so big. Tents and APCs. They must have strung out their bases around the mountain. The big guy leads me toward a single tent near a stand of trees and a long coil of barbed wire. He raps on the tent. Milan's head peeks through a flap, and it seems he is being born from canvas. He sees me and emerges.

"Jay, the weather was the same when we first met in Sarajevo."

"I remember."

The big man leaves us.

"I have learned not to feel the wet. I'm a magician that way. Come in."

The tent smells of socks and canned spaghetti. Milan adjusts the kerosene heater, and we sit on blankets. His sniper rifle leans near a postcard of Saint George and the dragon. Milan pulls a small bottle of plum brandy from his coat.

"For the bones," he says.

The rain on the tent sounds like the footsteps of gentle insects. I feel I could sleep.

"How are the fields back home?" I say.

"They burned some, but we protected most. One day,

our priest, you remember him from the church after our night in the rain, walked through the fields with incense to bless and purify. The guerrillas shot him in the leg, but he's okay."

Milan puts a charred coffee pot on the heater.

"Better than that tea shit you've been drinking with the other side."

"You know I have to wander."

"You are like a moth. From flame to flame, my mother used to say. Jay, you have any batteries? I was in the middle of Miles's *Bitches Brew* and my CD player died. I'm a piano player, but Miles pulled it all together around that horn. He made it all dance quietly around that horn. When I open my club after all this shit, I need to find a trumpet player."

I pull two batteries from my coat pocket, and Milan smiles.

"How big is this battle?"

"Just a skirmish on this end of the mountain. The guerrillas came down and tried to take a village. Dumb fucks."

"Why are you here?"

"To kill the man you want to interview."

Milan was called two weeks ago. The Serbs had their own spies in the guerrilla camp and decided it was time to shut down the jihad. Milan had been roving along ridges and through crevices looking for a bead. The dateman's patrols keep a wide perimeter, and Milan hasn't gotten close.

"Seen him?" he says.

"Not yet."

"I remember these guys from Bosnia. The 'muj' we called them then. Bearded nuts. I shot a few of them. All you can do is shoot them. They've crossed the line. I saw it in their eyes, their dead eyes. It's a part of nature we know nothing of. The Serbs, the Croats, and even the Bosnian Muslims here kill and rape and burn, but none of us is going to blow himself in two. Not even Milosevic is demented enough for that. What makes a man do it?"

The rain has stopped; snow blows through the tent flaps.

"It's my last war, Jay. My muscles are going. My eyes aren't so sharp anymore."

He's right. The young man inside him has gone away. The decay began outside Sarajevo years ago, his sniper rifle crossing his lap on that APC. It followed him into the psychiatric clinic and then home to his water mill and fields. He sought the simplicity of grinding wheat from the slow stone of his ancestors. He wanted to close his door and pull his fields in at night and sleep with his wife. He wanted to play his piano. But they came to him with stories of women nailed to barns and village burnings. There were more enemies to be killed, enemies to be killed from a distance, so they called him. His jaw is tight. He doesn't look slackened. His fatigues, his smell, his hands, raw and thinly furrowed, suggest his intimacy with nature, his understanding for the patterns and grooves of where he hides. His fingers, so tapered; they shimmer like seaweed beneath the surface, playing with jazz and titanium-tipped bullets in the mud of a mountainside. But he is right that his eyes are tired. I see they have lost a bit of that quick hardness. He showed me once how he shoots. The arc of the rifle butt snug on shoulder and high pectoral. The left hand cupped and firm below the barrel. The black barrel searching. The trigger finger frozen like a fish hook. The right eye squints into the scope. His breathing rhythm changes and finds unison with the target. They are one. A deep breath and a slow exhale and, before the second breath, the shot, the ripple through shoulder and spine, the powder smell like wisps from cap guns when I was a kid, and then the rifle down, the casing flickering to earth.

He turns the heat up and wraps a blanket around his shoulders. We drink coffee. We don't speak. The barrages near the mountain are further apart. The Kalashnikov fire comes in bursts and longer pauses. It is the sound of poorly trained men wasting bullets they do not have to waste. I lift the tent flap. MUP are gathering. A man on a stretcher is carried into a shack. Bandages speckle the mud. I hear a far-off helicopter. Milan's eyes are closed, but he is not sleeping. It's getting near dusk, and I have to go.

"So this isn't the big battle?"

"A mild tempest, Jay."

"When you going out again?"

"Tonight. I'll find the crack up there somewhere. It's patience and not minding the shit. They'll make mistakes. A Jeep will break down. A patrol will arrive late. Someone will take a piss at the wrong time. It's math. Spinning equations. Where you going?"

"I gotta go pick up my translator and another guy and try once more in mountains."

"You still have that young girl?"

"Yeah. Hey, Milan, don't make a mistake and shoot me up there. I'm the guy without the beard."

"I told you my eyes were going."

He laughs and holds the tent flap open.

"Jay, I'm gonna open that jazz club one day. No kidding."

He disappears into the tent. I hear batteries loaded and Miles Davis rising like a bit of lost music, drifting into the trees.

Snow blows, and the Leopard waits with Alija and Brian near the bombed wall of a farmhouse. The battle is dying. The MUP have pulled their units back toward their bunkers; tanks are netted in camouflage. The guerrillas are trying to slide past, and every few minutes the crack of a gun echoes with the false promise of something more. The Leopard looks at a map, but he doesn't need to; he knows what's out there in the near dark.

"Shit, Jay, thought we lost you," says Brian. "You get what we needed?"

"Yeah."

Alija stands near me, her face blushed with melting snow.

"The Leopard says we can get back up the mountain tonight."

"The problem is getting back down."

"This is true, Jay. How are you?"

"Your men seem scattered and confused."

"It was not a good day."

"How many?"

"Jay," says Brian. "We already have that. I'll fill you in later."

"I'm sorry about Vijay," says the Leopard.

"Did you know?"

"I only knew he liked to talk."

"We can wait another hour and take the Jeep up halfway and then walk. The fighting's done for tonight."

"Jay, I gotta file."

"We'll write now and file before we leave the Jeep."

"I'm checking on my men. I'll be back and we'll go."

Alija, Brian, and I sit in the Jeep. Brian's fingers are doing their tap dance over the keyboard. We write fast. If you can't write easily about battle, you have no business being in this business. A battle is concise, compressed, although I must admit casualty figures tend to be elusive. But all else is there, a grid of lines and rockets on a game board, shifting scenes of color, the battered, the smart, a whiff of analysis, a wink of foreshadowing, all taking shape in letters and strokes growing across the gray-blue glow of my eleven-inch screen. And then there's all that stuff that won't get in. That stuff you mark in the notebook to use later, but another day comes and more marked stuff gets added and there's little you can do except to keep writing and saving stuff because the fun is in the collecting.

"How many tanks, Jay?"

"I saw two."

"I saw three."

"I'm going with two."

"Why isn't it ever the same? Why can't two hacks in the same place come up with the same fucking numbers?"

"I left for a while. You didn't. You saw an extra tank."

"I know, but I'm a congruent guy."

"An obsessive."

"Ah, Alija makes a joke. I thought you were sleeping," says Brian, "Hey, Jay, how many words you write?"

"Nine hundred and sixty."

"I'm at a thousand ninety-nine."

"Okay, you win."

"Most of it's shit. They'll cut it."

The Leopard knocks on the window and slides into the Jeep. Strands of guerrillas are walking the mountain road. The wounded hang off stronger men. A few are draped over donkeys. Some of them try to hop on the Jeep, but the Leopard yells them off, and I lock in the four-wheel and up we go again into the black and snow and toward the stars, but the stars aren't out, only the moon, glowing like a slim white flame between passing clouds. The Leopard's mustache is not trimmed to its usual perfection. His fatigues are wrinkled; there's dried dirt on his face. His boots are scuffed, and he smells of damp leaves. We drive slowly. Three guerrillas walk in front of us; they seem like comrades from a picture taken long ago. They smoke and laugh and readjust their guns. We pass them, and they wave. Then there is a whine and the sound of tires grabbing loose earth. Three Land Cruisers veer down the mountain and slide around a curve about a hundred meters away. Lights off, they head toward us.

"Stop, Jay."

"What?"

"Stop. Get out now."

The Leopard hops out and stands in the road waving his hands over his head.

"Jay."

The Land Cruisers slow and then stop. The Leopard walks toward the first one. A window goes down. Alija can't hear what they're saying. Two men get out of the back of the Land Cruiser. Their stubby, Eastern European–made machine guns hang low on shoulder straps. Brian and I walk toward the Leopard, but the men with the guns, I can see now they have beards, wave us back. The Leopard leans into the window. Another door opens, and, in the interior light of the cruiser, I see him. His back is straight, but there is an underlying fluidity about him. His black eyes dart back and forth from the Leopard to the windshield. His beard stops at his sternum; bandoliers crisscross his chest, but, unlike most men arrayed in bullets, he seems compressed by their weight. He is willowy, cane-thin, a crack in a window. All energy is in the calmness of his face. It is sepia but not old. It is carved not in fine angles but in a long oval flow, as if its features were shaped from a desert. His hands, moving in the light, are supple. He pulls at his beard and laughs, and the Leopard laughs, and the men around him relax their trigger fingers and breathe in the snow and the night air. I wonder if Milan is out there peering through his scope. There is no shot, only the after-battle sounds of retreating steel and leather. The man slides out of the Cruiser. The door shuts. The light goes off. He stands in silhouette with the Leopard. A few minutes pass. The Leopard and the dateman come toward us. Alija steps near me. The dateman looks at the Leopard, and the Leopard guides Alija toward the Jeep.

"We will speak in English. Don't take notes. If you

write, you think of the shape of words but not their meaning. It is better just to talk."

"Who are you?"

"I won't give my name, but you know I am not from here."

"Where?"

"Sudan, Saudi Arabia, Afghanistan. All the places where our brothers struggle."

"What struggle?" I ask.

"Against you. The hand your government imposes through illegitimate regimes that rob our wealth and deny us honor and dignity. Why should a man hunger in the land of Allah? Why should God's face not shine on everyone? Why should we be at your heel, or the heel of your servant? Even your Jesus says beware the beggar at your table."

"You didn't mention Palestine."

"Palestine is the cause of all Muslims. It is understood."

"Why are you here? The U.S. is not helping the Serb government. It wants Milosevic out."

"The struggle is wide. We are against all the West. There is no difference between American and Serb. How naive of you to think the U.S. doesn't have a secret hand in keeping these people oppressed."

"I don't think Allah is on the minds of most men in these mountains."

"Allah's in every man's mind. We have come to show them."

"These men want only their lands."

"Some see larger things attached."

"Are you training suicide bombers?"

"We have only martyrs." He smiles. "Our languages are so different. They intrigue. Yours flows almost uninterrupted from chest to mouth. Ours is more complicated. It resides in many places, throat and nose and chest. We speak with our bodies. Do you understand? We will never be in harmony. Our words come from different places. I am speaking your language now, but you still cannot know my heart."

"Are you training martyrs in camps in the mountains?"

"We instruct young men on how to see Allah's face. What's that line in your Bible? It's a beautiful line: 'And the Word was made flesh.'"

"Why here?"

"This is the edge of Europe. Why should we not be here? Your infidel army is in Mecca."

The dateman doesn't raise his voice, wraps no wire around his words. Part of him sounds like a textbook fanatic, hitting all the familiar notes of radical Muslim rage and paranoia. But his flow is more natural, more controlled. One sentence glides into another and then another with no sting of emotion. He could be making a shopping list or instructing a child on the dangers of crossing a busy street. It is the timbre of the voice that evokes: it is smooth, not the quiet baritone I had expected; no, it is pitched more to the sound of wind through a bone, not a whistle but a long and resonating lilt. I've encountered only a few such voices. They invite you to crawl inside them, to be soothed.

"What did you do before this?"

"I'm an architect. I studied in London."

"What have you built?"

"Nothing, yet. I study cities. Glass, steel, and mortar. They are the imges of what we are. Our outside selves. Allah, of course, dwells within us. When I was a boy, I used to think buildings were only storage places for people. Things stepped into for work or prayer. My father was an engineer. Once he took me on a trip with him to Europe. I saw then that buildings are the collective art of a nation. Armies defend what architecture inspires."

He grins.

"You like precision and order."

"My father used to tease me that I had become a man of blueprints."

"Why is an architect in these mountains?"

"It is cold, and we have little time."

"You've mentioned Allah," says Brian. "The Koran is often ambiguous. You can twist it many ways."

"You Americans do the same with your Bible and Constitution. You want to build a shining city on a hill for the whole world. But it must be your city on your hill built by your architects."

"What happens now?"

"You have big guns. We have the martyr's will. We shall see."

"It looks like you're leaving."

"We have come to do what we could. It is now up to them."

"Why take off just as things are getting interesting?" says Brian.

"We have left instructions."

"Maybe you didn't get enough converts."

"Armies have converted here for centuries. The Romans, the Ottomans. It goes on."

"NATO may be the next army."

"They will come, of course, but they are another army of the past."

"The battlefield is changing?"

"It has changed."

A man whispers in his ear.

"I must go."

"Can we ride with you a bit to talk?"

"One day you'll learn my language, and we will talk more."

"One more question," says Brian. "Why did your men kill our friend Vijay? He was a Muslim."

The dateman doesn't answer. He slips into the Land Cruiser and, without lights, vanishes down the mountain with his small caravan.

"I'm gonna type this up before we forget," says Brian. "'Don't write.' I hate that. I hate that obscure, opaque bullshit. Changing battlefields. Cryptic one-sentence bullshit. He hasn't got it, Jay. He didn't ignite the fuse. That's why he's driving away."

"What'd you expect?"

"Something I can build a goddamn lede around. Blueprints and architecture. What the hell were you driving at? We had a few minutes with this guy, and you want him to wax eloquent about him and his daddy roaming around Brussels looking at gargoyles and cathedrals."

"I was looking for a way in."

"There's no way into that chamber except head on."

"You didn't get too far with your 'Koran is ambiguous' bullshit."

"At least it was on point."

"C'mon, man, the guy told us he wants war with the West."

"You know how many bearded wackos out there want war with the West?"

"Yeah, but how many are up here doing it? Of course he spoke in abstractions. That's what they do. You were hoping for a sound bite? These guys aren't about sound bites, Brian. You know that."

Brian storms off to the Jeep, unfolds his laptop, and slams the door, snow coiling in the whoosh of air.

"He didn't make it, did he?" I say to the Leopard.

"He got many, Jay," says the Leopard. "But not enough. A shallow root is maybe all he was after."

"How's he getting out?"

"Over the same mountain that brought him here."

"Did he come in with donkeys and dates?"

"Donkeys, dates, and a few Land Cruisers, but mostly bullets and money and a box of Korans. He also had a copy of the American Special Forces Handbook on covert military operations. It had been translated into Arabic, but the cover was in English. Where is Carlisle, Pennsylvania?"

Chapter 15

We drive to the guerrilla camp. Brian and I file our stories on the day's battle on what's left of the sat-phone battery, and we sleep in the same sheep shed we slept in with Vijay. Morning mist forms a seam between earth and sky, clear above us and snowing below. The Leopard brings coffee and then leads us to the dateman's compound near the mountaintop: three wood-and-stone houses and a small mosque spaced about thirty yards apart and hidden in trees form the points of a rectangle. Worn paths scraggle to each house, and bunkers, fortified with sandbags and booby-trapped with land mines, rim the perimeter. The Leopard nods toward the first house. He walks up the steps and opens the door. We enter a new world. A strange art faces us. Buildings are drawn on the walls as if someone, perhaps through a restless night but with tedious, cool efficiency, had dreamed up a city, an amalgam of architectural styles, and fused it into an intricate voice: the glass and angles of Japanese design, touches of neo-classical, a bit of gothic, a coil of postmodern, and a towering reach of slender structures shaped like steel arrows and slicing into the sky. Koranic verse is inscribed on some buildings, but it looks odd, the curls and half strokes of a misplaced hymn.

"No trees," says Brian.

"What?"

"Not even a date palm. No green. Can't live in a city with no green."

Through a door, a kitchen unfolds with kerosene stoves and posted lists of chores for cooks, dishwashers, servers, and "prayer sayers." Dish towels are folded and plates stacked amid the grit and scent of cleanser. The windows are small and spotless, and the wood floors are fresh-cut and speckled with amber pearls of sap. Off to the left, the Leopard opens another door to a room with a mat on the floor and a crate in the corner. There's a photo tacked on the wall of a boy with a man. Both are dressed in dark suits and glisten with the Vitalis haircuts of the late 1950s or early '60s. The man is tall and wears oversize black-rimmed sunglasses that seem to hover more than rest on his slender nose. He bends toward the boy, and his narrow tie hangs in permanent suspension, one of those odd images in a picture that reminds you photography is an eerie pause between two breaths, a kind of undetected death woven into what we like to think of as life's uninterrupted motion. The boy, appearing to be about ten, holds a map and is at once studious and happy against the right angle of his father's tie and what seems to be a blurred muddy river bending in the distance, or maybe it's a burst of dust snaking through a desert like in those old pictures of the Pyramids. The boy is unmistakable. He is the dateman.

"This was his room," says the Leopard. "It's empty except for this picture. Why would he leave this?"

I put the picture in my pocket.

"He was in a rush."

"He was too precise."

"You think he left it for a reason?"

"A taunt."

"Mystery."

"A clue."

"There's no TV."

Broken discs and smashed computers — their hard drives gone — are scattered over another room. A small pile of charred papers lies nearby. The second house is stacked with bullet crates and fuses and boxes that once held RPGs and mortars. A sign in Arabic and Albanian reads: "Keep your soul and your weapon clean." The third house is a large room with a chalkboard and the scent of gunpowder. On the left wall hang two posters of teenage boys, their faces serene, kneeling in fire and looking to heaven. A wind seems to be blowing through them, riffling their clothes and hair and lifting the flames through lines of Arabic writing I cannot read. Alija tries to decipher. Two vests lie on a desk. The Leopard examines one. It is thin, refashioned with strips of Velcro, and six pouches, the width and length of a ruler, are sewn on each of the front flaps. A wire drops from one of the pouches and at its end dangles a silver cylinder the size of a roll of pennies, tipped with a red button. The chalkboard is half erased, a blur and swirl of white, the shade of a swan's wing. Inside this blurry rage there is a bus full of stick people and a stick-person driver. Standing outside the bus is a figure more carefully drawn, wearing clothes and a button-up shirt. With two dots for eyes, a nose shaped like an upside-down 7, he is smiling. The Leopard lifts a notebook written in Albanian from the floor. He reads: "Act friendly, but not too friendly; act like you're going to the market. Be calm. Breathe slowly. Don't sweat. Sweat causes suspicion. Move to the middle. Feel the button on your thumb. The cause is just and blessed. Soon Paradise."

"Notes to live by," says Brian. "Wonder where these guys went."

"Nobody's here," says the Leopard. "While you were interviewing the dateman last night, my men told me this compound emptied. A lot of the fighters, including about forty Arabs, joined our units. The others slipped through the forest and disappeared."

The Leopard steps closer to Brian and me. He flicks to the back of the notebook. He looks at us and begins to read: "To the Great One, peace be upon him, my last will and testament. My name is Sena. I have a wife and a son and a small home near my father's house. The village elders should collect what they can of my body but leave it unwashed. I am a martyr, and the book says a martyr carries his blood and dust to paradise. He is purified in death. I did not know this. I did not know much before I came here. I lived in a world of my enemy's creation. I saw through the eyes he gave me. But I have new eyes, and I will destroy his world and strike at his heart. I am happy to scatter my body like rain. God's righteousness protects me. My brothers here know this too. Our army will flood the enemy. Be he Zionist or Christian Serb, they are all the same. They are sheep to be slaughtered.

I am twenty-four. I finished secondary school. I have few worldly possessions. My family may divide them as they see fit. To my father, I say I am willing to die and have no fear. To my mother, I say do not weep. To my wife, I say after some time you may take another man from the village, but only with my father's blessing. To my son I say the silver coin hidden in my shoe is yours."

The Leopard closes the notebook.

I can't wait any longer. It's time. I tell Alija her brother was here among young men like Sena. She looks at me and then to the Leopard, who shakes his head yes. Her face hardens. Its imperceptible lines pull tight, its eyes narrow. She steps toward me but turns away, like a bird that sees a spot on a window and, in a space of time too short to measure, flits sideways to avoid collision. She stands in the middle of the room, and again, like that time we visited her burned house, I think she'll break, but she doesn't. She breathes in. You can sometimes detect the spirit of someone who's been in a room, a lingering trace, a wisp, an odor, something. Alija searches the notebook the Leopard was holding, but the scrawled yearnings for eternity are from an unknown hand. She frisks the vests and their pouches; nothing of Ardian, only loose threads and gunpowder grains. She studies the squiggles and lines on the chalkboard, looking at each face on the bus and trying to look beneath the bus to what was written before. The room is sparse and stingy. It gives nothing, but she looks in the corners, on the walls, searching for initials, a strand of hair. She steps outside and walks toward the other houses. She doesn't rush. One learns not to rush in this country. The Leopard follows to keep her away from

the bunkers and land mines. Brian and I make notes and di-
agrams. The less there is, the more you catalogue. The sound
of battle drifts through the clouds and up the mountain to
the clear sky. It shimmies through me like familiar music, si-
lences expanding and contracting between notes.

"Jay."

Alija stands in the doorway.

"Come."

She leads me through the trees to two dirt humps near
a ridge. The Leopard stands with shovels.

"Dig, Jay."

The Leopard and I find a rhythm. The graves are shallow. The bodies are poorly wrapped and their skin is the
color of ink and milk. Alija gets on her knees and brushes
dirt off the face of the first one. He is maybe fifty. There is
no trace of blood or wound, and he seems oddly uncon-
torted. She moves to the second body. She brushes the dirt
again. The face is young. She stops. She wets her hands with
saliva and brushes harder. She stares into the eyes and the
mouth, half full of dirt. She reaches through the frozen hair
and lifts the head the way a rich woman lifts a vase. It is not
her brother. She moves her thumb over his lips and lowers
his head. She stands and walks away, dirt and a bit of blood
on her palms. It is not until we begin reburying the bodies
that I see the boy has no hands; they have been blown off,
and the bones at the wrists are splintered and sharp.

The Leopard pulls a folded piece of paper from the
boy's pocket. Another note: "To my God, peace be upon
him. I am Ahmed. This is not my land. These mountains I do
not know. It is cold beyond what I have ever felt. I am from

213

Saudi Arabia, from a village near Medina. It is a small village, and you would not know its name unless you were from there. I have come here to defeat the infidel. To die before him, so he can see the power of my sacrifice. I will turn to flame and smoke and blow through him. He is my enemy; for all time he is my enemy. The teacher here has taught us much. New worlds, new knowledge are open to me. I have no wife. I have no children. All I have to leave is my name on the wind. If you read this, please, dear brother, know that I have sacrificed for you. I have happily gone to battle for you, my unknown brother. If innocents should die with me, there is no worry, for they are martyrs too. They are blessed. Whatever God takes in righteous battle is pulled to God forever. Read my name upon the wind. Ahmed."

The Leopard and I cover him with dirt and tamp and smooth the grave; I don't know why. We search the compound again, looking for hidden storage bunkers, signs, scraps of some definition, a paper in the wind. We seek more writing, Arabic or not, some document of what happened here. A diary would be nice, something more precise than the notebook and fiery wills. Who are men like Sena? Like Ahmed? We have only bomb pouches and stick figures made of chalk. This is the sensation, but where is the gist? Where is the nut graph? Where is Ardian? Does he have his own note folded away in a pocket? His will and testament? What would he leave? His polished shoes, the ones I saw days ago in his burned bedroom? I walk back to the first house and stand before the city on the wall. It is finely sketched and seems to be floating, a mystical cobbling of lines and towers. The dateman's vision of Jihad City? Who lives in such a place? Or, perhaps, here, on this wall in the mountains, it's just a city of impermanence, a landscape to fade away or be painted over or destroyed by fire or a missile. I stare at it. I walk through its streets. Nobody is here. The steel and glass of a wild man's dream. Is he wild? I met him. He does not seem wild. He is calm and thin like a clarinet. Willowy. Speaking in obscurities and allusions. Why are the words of fanatics so imprecise? It's as if the pure definition of their cause eludes even them and they paper over the gaps with pretty things and fire. Alija comes in and stands beside me. We seem like two people in a museum who have wandered into a room others have just left, and for a moment we have the art to ourselves. She turns and stands before me. She says nothing but forces me to look away from the dateman's perversion and into her eyes, to make sure I understand the sin, the betrayal, of keeping a secret from a girl haunted by what lives in hidden places. She is angry, but, more than that, she is desperate and wanting so much to pull her brother from the designs and air around us. Ardian must have stepped on these floors, touched the chalk, kept a notebook, seen some vision, sketched his own city, but he has left no inkling of a direction for her to follow.

"You should have told me earlier, Jay."

"There was a lot uncertain. I was hoping . . ."

"You had no right."

"We'll find him."

"You had no right, Jay."

She wipes her eyes and pulls her face tight. Brian and the Leopard come in.

"We scoured the place," says Brian. "We found another

215

underground bunker. Probably for munitions. Freshly dug but empty."

"There wasn't that much up here, anyway," says the Leopard. "I visited twice before. It was sparse even with people. All you heard were whispers."

Alija stomps the wall twice with the bottom of her boot and walks to the corner. The Leopard follows, wraps an arm around her. She turns in to him.

"The war is coming, and Allah's boys have scattered," whispers Brian.

"What do we have here?"

"Let me give you the U.S. intel version: terror hive in faraway mountains. Shadowy figure escapes in Land Cruiser, leaves blueprint on walls."

"Bearded men, architecture, and bombs," I banter, to forget about Alija's eyes.

"Or architecture, bombs, and bearded men."

"You should end with the strongest word."

"Bombs would appear to be the strongest image, but bearded men is more poetic. It lingers longer."

"Carries you nicely into the next graph."

"Are we doing narrative or straight up?"

"Straight up."

"I don't like narrative anyway."

"You're too impatient for narrative."

"The more narrative you do, the more editors you deal with. Who needs that? I listened to a guy read his narrative 'reportage' at a conference once. It went on and on and on. He described the pictures on the wall, the color of the toilet, how many slices in the loaf of bread. I got a headache, so I put my hand up and asked this guy, 'What's the point?' He said, 'The point is I'm taking you to a place.' And I said, 'Yeah, but I don't want to be there, so what good is it? Just tell me what the skinny is.' And he said: 'That comes later.' I said, 'I don't have time for later. I don't care how many slices of bread are in the loaf. I just want to know if Johnny killed his mommy, or are you going to jerk me off for three thousand words?'"

"You have this hostile streak, Brian. And anyway, no one gets three thousand words anymore."

Alija walks along the wall again, looking down the avenues of the dateman's city. She is crying. A slow, quiet cry. Alija is good at binding sound; she stores it in her bones. The Leopard goes to the window. He smashes it with his gun and breathes the cold air that rushes in like wind through hanging laundry. I close my eyes and feel it, remembering linens ghosting in backyards; I remember: sheets billowing, shirts lifting, a strange bloom of snapping colors. I remember all that stuff years ago as a boy when things were folded and crisp and the best feeling of all was sliding at night into a bed of sheets still cool from the line. And then, late at night, sneaking out the bedroom window, dropping on a dewy lawn and racing up the sidewalk to meet my friends, older guys with paper routes and crumpled cigarettes. I'd help them fold and load their baskets. I'd shine their reflectors and send them peddling toward the lip of dawn. I'd walk home with a newspaper. The ink damp, I felt the news had just happened. I knew the stories of the world before anyone else. They slept, and I understood the troubles in faraway places, all those little foggy, sinister capitals. I knew presidents and revolutionaries; there was always a Castro story, always a bit of misery and rain from the Soviet bloc; there was polio and baseball and Bart Starr; there were union guys and murders and blood the color of ink, my ink, the ink that rubbed off on my hands as I flipped the pages back to the comics and then to the television section, where I'd check on *Sea Hunt* and those Cartwright boys. It was a world on paper, a compressed thing of wonder. There was no bargain like it — the planet in your hands for a dime.

The Leopard steps out the door and pulls me aside. Another paper unfolds. A map. His finger moves to red dots: Pristina, Belgrade, Novi Sad.

"Targets?"

"Yes. Young men blowing themselves up. These fanatics tried it in Bosnia, but it didn't work. Could it here? I don't know. Look at this brainwashing. These wills. They've crossed over to someplace beyond us. This country, Yugoslavia, it's not even that anymore. It's been broken apart, divided, piece by bloody piece. And this is the last piece, Jay. Who will win?"

We're rushing down the path and away from the camp. The Leopard is fast. He glides shadowlike over the rocks. Alija is behind me and then beside me. She doesn't say anything. She takes my hand and walks with me awhile, then lets me go and moves ahead. Farther back, I hear Brian's big boots scuffing. The four of us find a disjointed unison and appear at the ridgeline; clouds and clear sky battle. Night is minutes away, and guerrillas huddle in blankets. I unroll my sleeping bag in the sheep shed. The Leopard checks his men. Brian writes in the Jeep. He's beyond a thousand words and still clattering, hunched in the window like a card player contemplating a bluff. No matter how much he writes, no matter how much I write, the dateman is a bit of refracted light, a glimpse, not essence: a riddle of journalism. Think of the editor peering at his screen. What's he to make of this story? Bomb vests and Koranic verses, a stunted pattern implying something more. Yes, it will be noted. Of course it will be given words and a headline and noted. But the dateman is but a wrinkle in a larger set piece. The warplanes are parked and pointed, the dictator Milosevic slinks with brandy in his bunker, a draftsman down a corridor in a Washington basement ponders grids on a map. War in Europe. How can the dateman's jihad whispers and weird architecture compete with that? What media marketability does he have to dim the glamour of a Stealth Bomber flown by a young man from the middle of Nebraska, a guy with one of those American kick-ass smiles who's doing a live feed with Oprah about his impending mission across the dark Balkan skies? He calls her ma'am and everyone goes, "Ahhhh." The dateman was right to break camp and scamper. Why get creamed before your message gets out? Briefly chronicled but ultimately forgotten, a curiosity for arms merchants and Swiss bankers and those who know that the currents moving the world run deeper than images flickering across screens. He was here, he made a mark, but perhaps he is for another time. He is the laborer in the Bible, the farm hand in the Koran, dipping a hand in a sack, scattering seeds. Alija lies beside me. Her face is cool and smells of soap.

"Is there water?" I ask.

"A few bottles left in the Jeep."

"I haven't heard any gunfire in a while."

"The Leopard says they're not fighting tonight. I checked with some of the guys who came from the date-man's camp. No one knew my brother."

"How many Arabs did you see?"

"None. They must have gone somewhere else. The Leopard doesn't know either."

Alija's silhouette is sharp. She says nothing more. In all the time we've been together, our conversations have mostly been with, and through, others, with Alija the conduit, the alchemist turning two languages into one. She is my screen, my sieve, my word collector. I want her to whisper her secret to me again. I want to know more; I want her story to never end. It lies out there in remnants on a field of lightning and a galloping horse. She will never tell me all. I have been given images I can understand and process: rape, a dead boy soldier, escape. A tragedy in three acts. Language, this smattering of ink and sound, cannot explain all; there is a layer, an invisible space between syntax, that cannot be bridged. You can write poems on the pain of fire, but you know nothing of fire until you place your hand on the stove. I live in that vocabulary between poem and stove. I turn toward Alija. She kisses me. Perhaps I am forgiven. The tears on her face press to mine. She rubs them off my cheeks, and I feel like the young man in the grave. The one with no hands. She holds me, and I hear Brian outside connecting the sat phone to the Jeep's engine and cursing at one of his sources like some night bird cawing into the ether.

"My father painted houses," says Brian.

Alija sleeps; I stand with him near the Jeep.

"No ambiguity in painting houses."

"Not once you mix the color right. I worked with him in the summers."

"T-shirts and turpentine."

"It was good work. Every day you could see how far you'd gone. You finished one house and went to another. Thousands of miles of paint over a lifetime. I used to love his truck. It was battered, it stank and was cluttered with so much shit, from rollers to coffee cups to faded bills, that I thought all the world's lost things ended up in that white pickup. Sometimes I just want to paint a house, Jay. See something finished, complete, in the sun."

"Alija thinks her brother may have gone back to the university in Pristina."

"That kid will be screwed up no matter where he is. Let's drive her there tomorrow. I could use a scenery change, maybe look up my Russian buds. Wash some clothes."

"We may get cut off. May not be able to get back here."

"Ahh, and miss the little war on this freezing mountain. Jay, once the NATO boys start dropping the big hardware, these guerrillas won't mean shit. They'll duck and go along for the ride and pop their heads up when the ground settles and the MUP have scattered. We're looking at the big picture. The guerrillas get the spoils, and Uncle Sam does the lifting. Once the bombs start dropping, the story here is all about refugees."

"What, you're writing analysis pieces now?"

"I'd rather write an analysis than a narrative. You got any numbers of military-political experts I can call?"

"I don't use them."

"Everybody does."

"Why do I need to call a guy sitting in an office in Washington or in some university to tell me what's going on in the country where I'm sitting? Makes no sense."

"I never figured you for an expert hater. Is there something dark from your childhood?"

"I don't hate them. I just don't need someone to tell me that I'm in a shit storm when I can look outside and see it's brown and windy and stinky. 'Jonathan Yukityyuk, an international expert specializing in small, messed-up countries and based in a think tank buried in the ground somewhere in Maryland, said the Balkans are spinning out of control and that time will tell what the future holds for this perilous stretch of European real estate.'"

"I've got goose bumps."

"Mr. Yukityyuk, who has never actually traveled to the country in question, believes that no matter what happens Washington will have a mess on its hands for a long, long time. Oh, excuse us, Mr. Yukityyuk has to go now. He's just been called by *Nightline* to pontificate his expert wisdom into people's living rooms, a move that hopefully will prompt interested Americans into buying his latest book: *The Quagmire We Live in When We Blow Up Other People: A History and Litany of America's Overseas Engagements in Foreign Lands.*"

"I've read it. It's essential. I wish we had a dateman expert."

"Hasn't been invented yet, but soon they will be legion."

The Leopard walks up and leans on the Jeep. I study him. The Leopard. I love the name, a sleek beast from a distant geography. But his finery and perfections are diminishing. Tea stains his teeth. His fingernails are no longer compact moons. There is that quiet majesty, yes, that belief that man can change his circumstance. The Leopard is tired, though, his hands dirty, his boots battered. His fingers are nicked, and his nose is runny, a kid left too long on the playground. His maps don't crinkle anymore. They unfold like cloth, lines and elevations blurred. His men float below him, bobbing uncertainties in the cloud line, loading bullets and looking downhill to the Serbs stretched across the narrow valley. War is about stamina, not about death.

"Have you killed anyone yet?" says Brian.

"I don't know," says the Leopard. "I've shot into things that moved and then they didn't move."

"But you never saw."

"Never saw."

"How much does a bullet weigh?"

"A few ounces, maybe. Brian, you must have had a lot of bullets in your hands over the years."

"Yeah, but I'm not good at weight, or guessing ages."

"How old do you think I am?"

"Fifteen."

"Come on."

"I'm telling you I'm lousy at this shit."

"Thirty-four."

"A good age."

"Jay, is thirty-four a good age?" asks the Leopard.

"I met a woman once. She was thirty-four. She was

223

Egyptian, and we were the only two in a hotel somewhere in Algeria. A sandstorm came across the desert. Gusts blew through window cracks. It was dusk. The small hotel staff had retreated. She came into my room with silver spoons and tea made from black lemons. We sat and talked until morning. The storm passed, but the dawn was hazy. She kissed me, just once, and left. I heard her creak down the hall and go into her room. I heard her draw water for a bath, and I fell asleep near a plate of cut lemons. It was beautiful."

It's time to go. The Leopard gives us a guide to lead us down to the mountain and onto the hard road. Alija hugs the Leopard, and he shakes my hand and looks at me, water in his eyes from the cold air. He gives Brian a bullet. "Weigh it when you get a chance." I tell him we'll be back after our trip to Pristina. He says promises like that can't be kept anymore, no one knows what will happen, but perhaps one day we'll meet in a different place, a free country. He hands me a letter and tells me to give it to his family in the city. He hands me a photograph of the two of us sitting on a ridge. I don't know when it was taken. I don't know who took it. He says he has a copy, too.

"I think you loved that Egyptian girl," he says.

"It was a while ago."

"What do you remember most about her?"

"Her voice, and knowing I would never have it."

He steps closer.

"Whatever you write about the dateman, make sure you say he is not us."

We pull away. I see the Leopard in the rearview, his men beginning to gather around him. Instructions for a new, wet day. We come around the last mountain curve. The guide hops out and disappears into the skeleton brush. The Serbs are quiet across the valley. Brian counts their APCs. Alija puts on her MUP mask. We head toward another checkpoint in the rain.

Chapter 16

Pristina slumps like a kicked dog in the distance. No matter from what vantage point one approaches, the city never inspires, not even a swatch of charm, only grids and gray blocks from demented architectural minds. It is a place half finished, yet half dead. The tallest building is the Grand Hotel, a flimsy box of fake bronze and gold where the elevators stop midfloor and the staff wears shiny, worn tuxedoes, each at least a size too small. Even the diminutive bellboys walk around bound and shrunken by buttons and cheap twill. Their bow ties are cockeyed and frayed, like droopy black propellers. A tip doesn't raise a smile; everyone, it seems, is waiting for an RPG to whistle down a hallway, or for some suspicious-looking guy in boxer shorts and socks to be dragged across the lobby screaming, "It's not me, it's not me," before he's tossed into the back of a truck with crisscrossing-wire windows. If the Grand had a past opulence, it is strangled in the carpets that midday smell of feet and by evening emit scents of spilled drinks left by village couples on their wedding nights, who hurried and fumbled in narrow beds while downstairs gangsters in Macedonian black leather sipped Campari, which they didn't like but had been told was chic. One night, years ago, Leonard Cohen's "Dance Me to the End of Love" played in the bar, and a woman in a black-and-pink dress — sometimes they just appear like ghosts or lollipops — whirled alone over the floor in a broken rhythm that said, "I'm from somewhere in Eastern Europe, but, ahhh, I will try, and I will dance to the end of love or the end of hate or the end of whatever you want if you just put me in a car and drive me west, west to the sea." I bought her a drink and wished her luck. She disappeared hours later with a guy in a stolen Fiat with no plates, heading toward the mountains of Montenegro.

"I need to look for my brother, Jay."

"Jay, you think the Grand serves mousse? I could go for a good chocolate mousse."

"Will you come with me, Jay?"

"Jay, I'd even go for a Black Forest cake, nothing fancy."

"There's not much time, Jay."

The Grand is full. It's always booked until you slip the guy at the registration desk — the newly shaven one with pale cheeks and gray eyes, the one who smells of cologne rubbed out of magazine ads, the one who screws the maids in sunken hallways — a hundred-dollar bill, and then suddenly a room has opened up, another hundred and another room. Money is magic. We get in the elevator; for a moment we're suspended but not moving, like a knot in the middle of a tug-of-war rope. We click, shimmy, and rise. Fourth floor.

"Hey, Jay, do you have a doorknob?"

"Yeah."

"I don't."

Brian kicks open his door and laughs. Alija and I step into our room. Green-and-tan curtains. The toilet running. A few bugs in the sink. A cracked mirror, and that dim light, that fluorescent stain that follows you from shit hole to shit hole, as if the electricity is being strangled so it doesn't fully illuminate the things that lurk in the corners. The room is cold. The wool blankets have lost their itchy crackle. "Hold me, Jay." She steps into my arms. We stand at the window, watching snow the color of old nickels blow through the city. There are more MUP on the streets. The war has not come here yet. It is out there, hiding in the snow, obscured but moving closer, a tin and metal prattle on the distant outskirts. Alija steps closer to the window. She blows on it, and in the steam she writes. She blows and writes some more. The words vanish before I can read them, and I ask her what she's writing, and she turns and smiles and says nothing. The sound of traffic cracks and creaks, muffled by space and snow but lingering like an old woman's hum. I lie on the bed and close my eyes. Alija breathes. Her letters squeak over the window. I should call my desk, file the dateman story, write a memo, send something. Later. I start to drift. Alija sits on the bed. She takes my hand.

"Jay, let's go to the university and check on my brother. Maybe he came back, or maybe somebody knows something."

"Let me rest five more minutes."

"Why can't you sleep at night?"

"I don't know."

A knock. Who else?

"I have two lamps and no light bulbs, Jay. I'm in the dark."

"Is this literal or metaphorical?"

"It will be literal in a few hours. Now it's just unpleasant."

"At least there's still plumbing."

"Not for long."

"Give me five minutes, guys."

"C'mon, Alija, let's go look for my doorknob."

I hear their voices fade down the hall. I turn toward the wall. Painted beige cinder block. I trace the cracks. We need water, supplies, an extra car battery, blankets, socks, and cartons of cigarettes for the guerrillas or the MUP or whoever won't let us pass where we need to pass. The y key on my laptop is loose. The 2's not so good either, but numbers don't matter so long as there are letters. The sat phone needs a new cable, but if the war's not too long, we'll be okay. I should visit Vijay's grave, but there's no time. The dirt is probably not settled yet, a hump brushed with snow in a field of marble. It's a poor cemetery; there will be more wood than marble, split pine and oak markers laminated and lettered. I like it when the faces of the dead are chiseled on stones. Everyone is so handsome and pretty. The chisel men are paid extra; they are God. I cannot draw, but I wish I could take a line, bend it and turn it, make it go thin, make it go wide, let it curl and lift into something. I have words, and if I lose my y, I'll have twenty-five letters. I do hear stories, though. They shape me the way copper is shaped when it's hammered. The thoughts run. My stories are the memories of others. They fade over time. Parts of some get twisted into parts of others, dead faces scrambled and reassigned to different geographies, different wars. I say each time I will not let this happen. But it does. Sometimes when I read a story I have written years ago, it seems to have come from another voice. I can notice similarities in cadence and style, but I can't remember being there exactly at that time. The words, even the images, seem like someone else's. But I gathered them. I sifted them, put them on a screen. Only to — what? — have them lost to me? I used to keep clips of my stories. I don't anymore. They don't belong to me. They are just things out there, stuff I collected and sent through space, ramblings and facts taken from the lives of others. I am not a thief. For the most part, they were given freely.

It is dusk. Alija's brother is not at the university. No one has seen Ardian for months. We check some of his coffee shop haunts and Alija sees one of his old girlfriends. Nothing. He is traceless. Papers blow over the streets. We walk through the main square and pass the statue of the warrior on his horse. He looks like an Asian Viking, an oxidized bronze mix of Leif Ericson and Charlie Chan, Nordic or Slavic mingling with Far East. A king from some old world, or maybe the archetype for a new one. Who knows in this dark cold? His facial features, against this geography and population, seem like a painting hung in the wrong room of a house. He's a Rembrandt on a Picasso wall or vice versa, or maybe he's David amid the Cubists. But that's what you get when you're conquered, someone else's identity sitting high in the saddle. Alija points to what appears to be a gash of gold at the horseman's neck.

"My father used to say he bleeds sunlight. Some guys I knew from a village way out near the mountains drove here one night and tried to cut his head off. They sawed. They had power tools. We all watched. Sparks flew. They worked for a while, but that head wouldn't budge. The police came and all of us ran. One of the guys got shot in the leg, but he kept running. Two days later, in a creek, police found the big, carved head of someone who looked more like us. They covered it in a tarp and buried it somewhere."

I make a note: a nice metaphor, I suppose, for one of my stories. It's nice to be walking in a city again, even if it is this one. People moving like cutouts in windows, creeping behind shades, fuzzy, lights flicking on, little kids running down halls, clattering in stairwells and into the night, looking for Dad, whirling around him like dust, leading him home to dinner, yanking his hands and laughing that Mom is going to kill him. Kill him again for being late. We stop at a black-market CD shop. A guy with a shaved head rises and hugs Alija. They talk. I flick through titles, a hodgepodge of genres, Prince, Creedence Clearwater, Sting, Dire Straits, the typical classical selections, obvious jazz, two or three New Age albums, a Hank Williams and a vintage Black Sabbath, long before the days when Ozzy went nuts with rings and mascara. I wore my *Paranoid* album out as a kid. Ozzy was a screech and howl from another world. "I Am Iron Man" with that wah-wah guitar and the guys in the band standing in that field on the cover like drugged wheat with clunky belt buckles and boots. Rolled my first joint on that album cover. Me and Nut Johnson. Sprigs and seeds mostly. We barely got high, but we pretended we were as stoned as Ozzy himself, jumping on our spider bikes and riding to the cul-de-sac to hunt lost balls in the storm drains. Alija taps me and we go. There is no moon and no snow.

"That guy any help?"

"No. I'm still pissed at you, Jay. You never told me about the camp until it was too late."

"What could we have done? Gone up and knocked? The Leopard was trying to find out."

"But you didn't tell me. What if I didn't tell you, Jay? What if I left out a line of description? What if I left you with a big bubble of silence? Nothing to feed your notebooks. None of those details you like so much. What if I gave you only sounds, Jay, sounds you couldn't twist into words?"

"What now?"

"I don't know. No one has seen him."

"Would he have gone to your parents?"

"In that refugee place? No way. He would have come here."

Gunshots burst from a few blocks away. Nothing major. A guy's probably oiling his AK and waiting for war to come down his alley. Alija keeps moving. I follow. Her hair is nearly invisible in the night. We stop at a pizza place owned by a fugitive Bulgarian who sells guns out of the back. The guy shrugs. We walk to the mosque and wait outside the courtyard wall. A man with a cane and a milky blue eye comes out. Alija collars him. The man has heard about boys coming down from the mountains, but he hasn't seen any. He says there are many rumors and you can take your pick, but there is only truth and that is Allah. Alija asks whom she might talk to about the boys. The man says the world is big and boys can hide. Alija presses him, and the man says talk to Allah. Alija says she needs to talk to someone in town about the boys. The man says Allah is in town, and that Alija, although she is a woman, might find him if she is quiet and careful not to let the MUP follow her. The MUP are everywhere, but they don't see like Allah sees. They miss things, but Allah misses nothing. Allah's gaze, says the man, is like water in a room; it goes everywhere, fills everything. The man says you cannot look at Allah; you have to speak with downcast eyes. The man looks around. He says he has spoken too brazenly. He walks away, his cane clicking along the wall.

"I'm guessing he meant *Allah*, as in 'The Allah, peace be upon him.'"

"He did."

"If he's in town, maybe he's at the Grand."

"In a room with no doorknob."

The bar is full, and Brian and his two Russian journalist buddies are building a toothpick city between beer bottles.

"Nothing."

"Don't worry, Alija, he'll turn up. Meet Boris and Anton."

"Wodka?"

"Why not."

Boris is sleepy-eyed and Anton is wired; both are

stained by cigarette smoke, yellowed dolls with unruly hair. Russians are cool that way. They can go and go and go with no sleep. They are the last ones to go home unless there's a woman involved, but I suppose that's true of just about anyone once a woman crosses the threshold. They are talking about fishing and why Brian uses flies, a flicking wrist, and a whole lot of effort when all he needs to do is hurl a stick of dynamite into the river and watch fish float to the top. Boris and Anton laugh, and Boris stands up and does a lousy fly-fishing imitation. Brian looks like he wants to punch the Russians for such sacrilege; he says a fish needs to be caught with skill, says there's honor involved. Boris says it is a skill to keep a fuse lit till the very last moment before the dynamite sizzles in the water. Brian knocks down Boris's toothpick building. Boris knocks down Brian's. Anton orders another round.

"How you doing, Anton?"

"Have flu. Feel like dick in cold water."

"That bad."

"Worse, really, I tell you, worse. This flu on my head like two pieces metal pushing on brain."

"Too bad."

"What can do?"

The bar is a murmur. It's crowded, shoulder to shoulder, but words are moving beneath currents, whispers in a chorus before the conductor arrives. The happy anticipation of war is gone. The gunrunners, the pimps, the drug dealers, the profiteers, they're all worried now, plotting about how and when to get out with their fortunes before the bombs drop. They sit and hunch, draped toward one another, but not quite trusting one another, money hidden deep, pencils scratching paper, numbers traded, maps drawn. These guys are like blackbirds. They'll be in the air, vanished at the crack of the first shot. They're drinking heavily, and their women are wondering who's making the trip out and who's getting left behind. There's mud on the floor, and the waiters, their trays tarnished and sticky, don't seem to care about the broken vases on the tables and the flowers scattered near the door. The beer is cold, but there's no Beck's anymore. There's a squeeze at the border, that jagged line of barbed wire and gray light one hundred kilometers away. Alija sits next to Brian and the Russians, a fairy-tale damsel, I suppose, and I want to hold her and dance with her, I want to do that even though there's mud on the floor and I can't dance and the place is too gruff for tenderness, but I want to dance to something slow with this girl I sleep with but do not know, this spirit with things hidden deeper than a gunrunner's money.

I take her hand, and we dance. Brian and the Russians clap, and then that fades and the gangsters looking turn away. We dance, our boots sliding in slow circles, our hips pressed, Alija's head on my chest, like it is when we sleep, but we are standing and dancing and her hair is brushed and cool and it smells, I think, of apricots and rain, yes, that's it, apricots and cold rain blowing through a field. I can barely hear the music, the song I do not know, but it whispers and the bar murmur arcs over it and it seems at once intimate and lost, as if we are dancing in the living room of a house of strangers. I pull Alija close. I feel her grip around me, and for a moment we move in effortless symmetry, the way an unexpected breeze lifts the colors of a flag. She reaches for my hand, and we go to our room. We undress and slip into bed. I feel the cold bottoms of her feet, her hair dusting my shoulders and chest, and then quiet on the border of skin and bone. There will be no story tonight, no peeling back, no visit to the horse in the field or the men in her kitchen; we listen to nothing, and for a long time there is no sound, no rustle from the world, and then, snow, a dry snow tapping the window. Alija sleeps, her arm across me, over the blanket and cool. I get up and walk to the window and see my reflection, a gauzy presence drawn with an unsharpened pencil. I know the features. They are me, but they are the unfinished me. I step closer and come into a bit more focus, but I seem insubstantial, a blur hovering over streetlights. I should click on my computer and write. My notebooks are pleading for release. Tomorrow. Tomorrow I'll write long. File a big Sunday piece for the desk. They'll be happy, get some art, nice graphics, roll my words into a grid. Then everyone can go home and we'll do it again the next day, and the editors will say how about some more analysis here, a speck more color there, did he really say that? what's an RPG? we're opening up pages, we want to do this big, this is history, man, history, it's epochal. No, it's not. It's just another disturbance on the page.

I lie back down. I close my eyes, breathe with Alija's rhythm, and feel as if I might float into sleep, but sleep is a rim beyond. I dream awake. Where has the dateman gone? Over the mountains, vanished, folded into a fanatic's poem. Morning is out there, a distant slow swirl in the sky coming toward me. I know more of the sky than most. I watch it like TV, the plots and the subtleties; stars pull away and comets flare and the moon shimmers incandescent but elusive, a coin from God's pocket. A missionary in Africa told me once that the planets and the moons were God's spare change. It's kind of a weird image, but it works in the jungle. Not here, though; the sky here is shrunken and less ancient, unable to conjure the mystery between the mortal world and the cosmic. God's pocket is a step too far, too purple for the paper, but I could get the rest in, hide it in a graph between troop movements and mass graves, slip it into the copy so no one would see. Who would notice an inlaid astronomical observation? Little victories against readers and editors are essential.

Morning arrives, raw but sunny, a bit of ice melt on the hills. Alija wakes and smiles. The sleep wrinkles on her face will fade before she slips into the shower. Youth. She's quickly in and out of the bathroom, naked and dripping, toothpaste on her lip, a comb sliding through her hair. She turns, and I see the raised letters on her back; they are whiter, harder than the rest of her. Another stroke of the comb, and they disappear.

"No hot water."

"Surprised?"

"You never have knots."

"Knots?"

"Your hair. It's always smooth."

She jumps back into bed and covers me. Her brother is not found, so she is not happy, but there is acceptance, as if somehow in the night she had looked upon the bruises and graves of this land and reconciled things. Not to the point of forgetting, or calling off her search, but to contemplate possibilities she had kept closed before. Like an animal, she knows she needs her energy for the coming war. Brothers, after all, have been known to reappear. They've been plucked from earthquakes, pulled from the sea. What else does she have except hope? She kisses me, a wet snap of a kiss, and I can taste the water and minerals from her hair, feel the clean, cold squeak of her skin. She hops back out of bed and dresses. She is so young; sometimes I see how young she is, pressing against another morning, her words and her voice my only certainties. I do the shower spin, pull on my jeans and shirt, and follow her into the hall, where Brian is kneeling in front of his door with a screwdriver and two Russians.

"We found my doorknob. Anton passed out on the floor, and when he woke up he spotted it under the bed."

"You look a little pasty, Brian."

"Too much booze. I'm officially on the wagon. Hey, Jay, come here."

Brian and I walk down the hall, and Alija heads to breakfast with Anton and Boris.

"Tonight, Jay, eight o'clock."

"What, dinner?"

"War. There was a British spook drinking way too much last night at the bar."

"Who?"

"You remember that guy from Sarajevo years ago? The funny looking one with the bent nose? Him. He was whispering to some Brit hack. They were both wasted, Jay, but you know this guy; he's usually right. I called my office.

They're hearing similar shit. People seem to be moving faster and quieter in Washington."

"How are you on money?"

"Not good," says Brian.

"We've only got two flak jackets. Alija's going to need one. We'll stop at the black market after breakfast. We're going to need gas, a lot of gas, and we're going to have to hide it somewhere. Food too. I thought we'd have more time. The y key on my computer's not going to make it."

"Where do you want to be? The MUP are going to seal the place."

"We're going to have to hide the sat phone too. That's the first thing the MUP will go for."

"Think they'll arrest us as spies?"

"They'll probably kill us," I say.

"They won't kill us. They're going to need stories coming outta this place. Otherwise it's a black hole and NATO can do anything they please. Nah, the MUP are going to want this chronicled. They'll corral all the hacks. Maybe we should go back to the Leopard."

"I don't know. What do we get there? Guerrillas fighting MUP? The real show's going to be at the borders. I think you were right; it'll be an air war we can't see and hundreds of thousands of refugees we can. If we only have one choice, which we do, I say we go with the refugees and burning villages."

"You sound like *Jeopardy*, man. 'Alex, I'll take refugees and burning villages for two hundred.' Maybe we can backtrack to the guerrillas. There's going to be a lot of nasty shit between them and the MUP."

"I need socks."

"We're going to have to stockpile water."

"You're not bringing these Russians with us?"

"Screw them. They don't even know how to fish."

Brian and I go to breakfast. The Russians have vanished. Alija sits alone, squeezing brown from a tea bag and cursing the lukewarm water in her cup. We tell her.

"Jay, I need to look for my brother one more time. Today, here."

"Okay, Brian and I will drop you closer to the main mosque on our way to the black market. It's really happening, isn't it? This is the day the people here have wanted for so long."

"Be careful what you wish for."

"No, Brian, that's not true. You'd have to have wished like we did to know that that's not true."

"At least you got a dance in."

She smiles.

"If only we'd had a piano player in the corner," I say.

"In a white jacket," says Brian.

"Jay, if we find Ardian, he can come with us, right?"

"He can babysit Brian, keep him on the wagon."

"I want a real coffee," says Brian. "What's so hard about a real coffee? These are modern times."

We walk through the lobby. A guy sits bent over an espresso and a paper. Black leather and a dour mood; he looks like a bodyguard or some kind of backup for something going on upstairs. A wire-service photographer rushes out of the elevator, his cameras hanging off him and jangling like dull chimes. He owes me money, but I can't remember from when or where. The big war is landing tonight, and the bellhops and the concierge have no idea. They don't know our secret. They sense something has shifted, some twist in the air, but they don't know; they just feel that today, for the first time in a while, seems different than yesterday. We step outside. The sun on my face cajoles me into thinking I'm not here. The Jeep is so streaked with mud that I've forgotten what color it is. Alija hops in the front, Brian in the back, I'm at the wheel: our little family, each with his or her assigned roles. We're off.

"Jay, we gotta wash this thing. It's starting to smell in here. There must be an old banana under the seat."

"Alija, where do you want to go?"

"A few blocks up, and then you guys turn left to the black market. Jay, get an extra flak jacket in case we find my brother."

"Meet us back at the hotel. Then Brian and I are going to see a spook friend of ours."

"Hey, Jay, we gotta write some B matter too. Need some stuff in the computer to put under the lede in case we need to file fast."

"Jay, stop. Stop, Jay!"

"What?"

Before she answers, Alija's out of the Jeep and running toward the café on the corner. It's a half-lit place with clean windows, a multicultural den of old magazines, piano sonatas, and a first-rate espresso machine, where out-of-uniform MUP, Albanian intellectuals, NGO types, hacks, and Western spies pretend that life is fine and everyone gets along and if every place could be like this place — a MUP passing

241

the sugar to some dark-skinned kid with a false smile — then the world would be just grand. Alija rushes through the door, and I see him standing at the counter. He's lean. His hair is shorn; he's a coarser version of the boy in the picture Alija carries in her pocket. It's him. Ardian. I see the back of her as she hurries through the crowd toward him. She opens her arms, a bird at the brink of flight. I can only imagine the expression on her face. The journey ended, the search over, her brother, the polisher of shoes, the beaten boy, found. Ardian steps toward her. There's no warmth on his face, only eyes registering recognition, but it is barely even that. He knows her but he doesn't, squinting as if someone from long ago, a vaguely remembered face, appeared unexpectedly before him. He freezes for a moment and then lifts his arms to embrace his sister, but that is not what he is doing. Through his sleeves and through his open coat I think I see wires, and my eyes move toward his hands, and I see, on the left one, a cocked thumb. Then there is that pause in the world, that strange gap of immeasurable time. I feel the heat before I hear the sound, smoke and glass and then limbo, strangely soothing, a numb blindness until what's knocked out of you comes back. I open the door and run around the Jeep and see blood, bits of teeth, broken cups, glinting, twisted spoons, a finger, and the shred of a vest like the one we saw in the dateman's camp hung near the book of stick-figure drawings of men on fire. The heat seeps into my nose, grows heavy in my lungs. There's ash and sugar beneath my feet. Every sound seems as if it's reaching me from miles away or like the muffled voices of childhood traveling through a tin can and a string. A man with blood on his face lies on the sidewalk,

242

vegetables and streaks of milk around him. A woman with torn stockings and a twisted foot, the ankle exposed like a fleshy white knuckle, crawls toward a baby stroller with no baby in it. I check Brian. He's lying in the backseat, dazed but okay. I turn toward the café. Flames like filaments lace through black smoke, and then the smoke rolls and whirls. I run toward the café, but the heat is a wall and my face burns and I stand there looking in, the smoke playing magician tricks with my eyes, and I see two men sitting at a table, charred and slumping, white wisps rising from their clothes and disappearing into the black. I see a hose and water and people running and blue lights and MUP pushing people back and the sounds of crying and the flame shrinking and hissing and the black smoke fading to gray and the skeleton of the café exposed and nothing in the place where Alija stood. Where is she? I turn away. I close my eyes and breathe in. A boy tugs at me but sees I am not who he wants; he steps over a coat soaked with water and blood and disappears down the sidewalk. Two tires on the Jeep are flat. The headlights are shattered. I gather Brian. He has a few nicks on his forehead, but the blood is light, almost dry. "Alija?" he says. He looks past me. The smoke is turning yellow-gray. The fire is nearly out; hoses slide and curl like snakes. "Alija?" he says. He leans on me, and we step toward the café and look through to the blown-out back wall, its bricks a ragged frame to an alley where more wounded stagger through falling cinders. He says nothing more. We turn and rush over the curb and across the street. Sirens, footsteps, shrieks mingle in a messy finger-painting of sound; none of it's distinct, it's as if we're swimming through an echo. We reach the

Grand. The lobby lights surge and dim. The concierge and bellhops huddle around the front desk, counting money, pushing keys across marble. A man in a gray suit guards the safe. He looks like an ethnic cleanser from another era, older now and pressed into less vigorous tasks that call for fronting a sneer and keeping a hidden finger on the trigger of a Glock. Bartenders, sweating in cheap white shirts but their bow ties tight, hurry back and forth from the kitchen carrying sandbags and stacking them by the door. The café is empty, half-drunk espressos and cappuccinos dot the tables, and the Muzak, oblivious to the changed mood, plays like a misplaced interlude, a tinny string of false notes. A truckload of MUP arrives. Two of them hop out and haul a crate of grenades behind the front desk. Others run for the stairs to take positions on the roof. Hacks scatter through the lobby, conferring, sharing assumptions, calculating where to be next in a stream of what-if scenarios. It's like a weird sales convention for the dirty, the unshaven, the intrepid, and the lost. It comes now, the pulse, the charged air, the waiting for the when. An explosion can do that. Brian sits on a couch and reaches for his notebook. He looks at me, says nothing, starts scribbling. A man with a bloody child in his arms walks to the hotel window. He lays the body down and falls to his knees. The boy must have been killed in the blast. The man strokes the boy's hair; he cries out but no sound comes, a wail as hollow and hushed as a cave in a forest. TV cameras appear one by one and then clatter into a crowd of lenses zooming and widening; the click, the insect whir, and the cameramen, engaged in their own little war of elbowing and shoving, bend and contort to get the best picture they can of a fresh kill. The boy's legs are gnarled, curled; his arms skin-ripped and showing bone; his face, eyes wide, angelic and gashed, heaven skimming hell—dead. The man scoops up the body and turns. The boy's feet and head sway, a puppet being put away for the night. Blood trails the man. He turns a corner.

I walk upstairs and open the door. It is as we left it. Computer on desk, coins for the maid, a bag of gumdrops, a towel coiled and damp on the floor, the curtain closed, the comb on the bed, the bed still wet from when Alija jumped under the covers with me after her shower. I sit and trace the outline of her body, so small, slender, like a drawing from a sketchbook. She is here. I see her socks in the covers, strands of hair on the pillow, all the little clues that make a life. I reach for the towel and breathe her in, clean, a riddle of elements. This room is alive; it hasn't yet entered the day. It slumbers, waiting for light. It is hours behind. We are dancing. Boots untied by the window, noises in the hall, the creak of a far-off closing door. We are watching the falling snow; the cold, frozen country beyond us, wrapping us in hills and mountains. It conspires and whispers with us. The land gives, the land reclaims; we have seen it with others but not with us. Alija laughs and kisses me. We are in bed. She holds my face in her hands and slides alongside me. She breathes into my ear, and, with a finger, carves my profile from the night. She moves over me and settles on my chest, listening to my life, a thrum beneath bone. I roll toward her; she opens her arms. She laughs again, sweet and raspy, a girl fighting sleep. We are together, not because she is young and I am old, or because she is beautiful and I am not, but because we are damaged and we understand. We are sleeping. I, who could never sleep, am sleeping in her arms, and in the quiet, I hear a voice.

"Jay, let me tell you the story."

Syllable. Word. Inflection. Nuance. Paragraph. Life.

I sit up. The room and the day are one. I pack my things and reach into the shower for the small bottle of shampoo. It is the last scent I have of her. Apricots and rain in a field. I dry the bottle and seal it. I slip it into my bag next to the roll of undeveloped film I keep from another war.

The missiles come at 8:13 p.m. on a night of scattered clouds, a light breeze out of the southwest.

Chapter 17

"People insist that Macedonia is beautiful, but I don't think so."

"Rolo. What are you doing here?"

"This is an airport, Jay. I'm flying out just like you."

"It's over."

"Seventy-eight days and billions of dollars later."

"When did you get out?"

"A few days ago. Took a little R and R with a couple of hooker twins. They told me they were twins, anyway. How about you?"

"Came out this morning."

"In the whole time, huh?"

"At the border mostly. Sometimes we got in to see the MUP and guerrilla show in the hills, but it was bullshit. Too much NATO hardware flying through the air. How about you?"

"Jay, you keep forgetting our relationship. I can't tell you where. I'm a spook, man. Here, take this glass."

"Duty free."

"Irish whiskey."

"You gonna open it now?"

"Is there ever a wrong time to open Irish whiskey?"

"It was long, wasn't it?"

"Way too long. Hey, where's Alija? I'd figured for sure you'd be taking her out."

"She's dead, Rolo. You remember the café bombing in Pristina?"

"The morning it all started? I heard about it, but I was in the mountains. It was one of the dateman's boys, right?"

"Her brother."

"Jesus."

"That was the only one, too. All the other dateman boys scattered."

"It's a sin, Jay. I'm sorry. She was lovely. Did you write about it?"

"Yeah, I wrote about it. Paragraph twenty-six, forty-three words. It could have been the lede if the war had waited a day. I miss her voice. I danced with her, Rolo. The night before, we danced."

"Never figured you for a dancer."

"I did okay. What's your prediction for Kosovo?"

"NATO sits on it for a while, keeps the peace. Independence. Then another war. It's the Balkans, after all." He takes a long sip of whiskey. "Here's something that might interest you. Somebody took a shot at the dateman."

"Bullshit. I was with him in the mountains right before he left."

"Yeah, I was tracking him. After your little roadside tête-à-tête he kept heading south."

"Was it you?"

"No, I was just shadowing. I mean, I would have liked to have shot him, but I didn't. His Land Cruiser was coming around a bend. I could see it in my night-visions, and then, just before starting up another hill, pop, pop. The Land Cruiser braked, then it swerved, straightened out, and was gone."

"Did either bullet hit?"

"I doubt it. Too bad. Would have been a hell of a shot at night on that terrain. The sniper, whoever he was, could have saved us a lot of trouble. It's still something, though, isn't it? Someone else trying to take care of a problem you don't know quite what to do with yourself. A fascinating place, the world. That's me. They're calling my flight."

"Where's he now?"

"We're tracking him, Jay. You know, you've gotta have more faith in the U.S. government."

"But where is he?"

"You keep asking these sensitive questions. My flight's to London. Then who knows? But I hear the place to be begins with an 'A' and ends with a 'stan.'"

"Have fun, Rolo."

"One day, Jay, I'm going to write all my adventures down. You'll be in there."

Rolo waves and pulls his ticket from his duffel bag.

"Who was that?"

"Jesus, Brian. Why so long?"

"Don't give me shit, Jay. The line was endless. Nobody was taking bribes. I had to wait. Who was that guy?"

"Some aide worker from somewhere. I couldn't remember."

"Is that whiskey? Give me a sip. Two tickets to Vienna, my friend. Civilization. They have tortes in Vienna, right? I want a torte, Jay."

"I could have a torte."

"Then I'm going fishing."

"You going to call your desk?"

"Jay, don't bring editors into this."

The plane is crammed with unshaven faces and duty-free bags. We lift through a low roll of clouds and the sky clears and we keep rising, a bit of sun on the wing. I look out the window and see Alija's horse galloping across the blue. She will never catch him. Nothing was ever found of her; no bone, no fragment, no gumdrop, no ring. She vanished in the ash. I keep thinking about the scribbled last will and testament we found in the dateman's camp before the war. "If innocents should die with me, there is no worry, for they are martyrs too. They are blessed." The flight attendant brings whiskey. I reach for my notebook but slide it back into my pocket. I am scoured of words. The plane levels, and soon we will be in Austria.

Chapter 18

Now you know. Things happen. They connect. They come toward you from places you never considered, from mountains you never peered into, from funny-looking names you skipped over. Their prattle is discordant. They are small. They are only words and momentary images. Until they sit in cockpits and skim the morning horizon, closer and closer they come. I am in Baghdad with a new translator. He is a man with a missing thumb, but his English is good, not perfect, not like Alija's, but good. We struggle over precise meanings, and he whispers to me that sometimes there are no words for the things people tell him. When he goes for tea, I daydream. The Leopard is buried not far from Vijay, his mustache chiseled in stone by those men who make the dead pretty. Milan played jazz piano in Belgrade for a while. He disappeared about a year ago after calling to tell me that his hands often lost their way over the keys and that he couldn't trust them anymore. Brian, the last I heard, was fishing a river in Afghanistan. Megan was there too. No word from Rolo, but I imagine I'll get to wherever he is at some point.

Acknowledgments

I thank my agent, Sorche Fairbank, for her wisdom and tenacious spirit, and my editor at Arcade, Cal Barksdale, for his keen eye and thoughtfulness. I am also indebted to the tireless, inspiring tribe of war correspondents.